SICILIAN MURDER

A JILL QUINT, MD SERIES MURDER

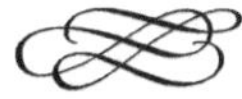

ALEC PECHE

Thanks to my friends for a delightful vacation on the island of Sicily several years ago. It's an amazing and historically significant island with ancients ruins representing the many peoples that have inhabited the island over the centuries.

Thanks to my first readers GM and KP for helping me polish this manuscript.

CHAPTER 1

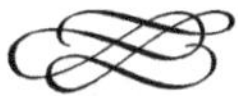

Marie Simon was sitting at a table for four, waiting for her friends to arrive for lunch. She was a little early and so took a few minutes to catch up on her email.

She saw an email from her sister with the subject line of 'need help'. Marie was one of seven children and this sister never asked for help. She clicked on the email wondering what was wrong?

'As you know, I'm on the island of Sicily, and my boss Randy Chen has been found dead in one of the craters at Mount Etna. I mentioned, to his daughter, the work that you and your friends do, and she would like to hire your team. How soon can you get to Italy?'

OMG! Marie thought and took a quick look at when the email had arrived in her inbox. Three hours ago. She looked at her watch calculating the time difference. It was a six-hour time difference between Italy and Wisconsin. Did her sister have her phone with her and what was the reception like wherever she was located? She dialed the number but it went to voicemail. Marie tried to remember what Brenda said before she left for the trip, but couldn't think of anything significant. She sent her a text and a longer email, grateful that she had arrived early to the noon lunch.

She dialed Jill's number for lack of anything else to do it the moment.

"Hey Marie, how's it going?"

"It's good. I'm at a restaurant waiting for friends to arrive for lunch and I got a weird email from my sister, and I thought I'd give you a heads up."

"Is someone dead?"

Marie exhaled a quick laugh and said, "How did you know?"

"Is the body in Wisconsin? I always enjoy visiting you guys!"

"Yeah and we enjoy having you here! The dead man is in Italy, specifically Sicily."

"We've never had a case in Italy. That could be interesting. We'll have to deal with the local police and depending on which way the case goes perhaps Interpol," Jill mused.

Marie noticed her friends approaching and waved to them.

"He was found dead in one of the craters at Mount Etna," Marie told Jill. Her friends startled at her words and then surmised who she was talking to and why.

"I'll have to study the volcano. Do you know if he died by falling or is that volcano strewing ash and poisonous gas at the moment?"

"Brenda didn't say, and I've been unable to contact her just yet. She did say that the daughter of the dead man wanted to hire us. Are you able to leave immediately if I get the call?"

"The daughter will need to sign our usual contract, but yes I'm able to travel immediately. I'll look into flights from San Francisco and know what my options are by the time you call back. I've been thinking about planting a grape that comes from Italy and so I might tag that on to the backside of our trip there. Knowing Nathan's love of Italy, I'm betting he'll join us there. Will you keep Jo and Angela informed?"

Nathan Conroy was the love of Jill's life and a master wine label maker.

"Yes, that sounds like a plan, I'll call you when I have more information."

Marie ended the call and looked at the three friends who had been shamelessly eavesdropping on her conversation. She grinned and said, "Well, a phone call like that is how our cases begin. I'm thinking Italy might be in my future if Brenda needs me there."

"Brenda? How is she involved in a case in Italy?" asked Jody who knew all of Marie's siblings.

"Her boss, Randy Chen, was found dead in a crater of the volcano on the island of Sicily. Likely the two of them were there sourcing new ingredients or visiting stores that sell their products. It sounds very bizarre to me and that was Jill, our team leader, forensic pathologist, private investigator and all-around friend who organizes these cases for the rest of us. She's ready to hop a plane to Italy as that is how the business works for her. When she gets a call for a new case, she has to be prepared to be there in say thirty-six hours. So she's used to dropping everything and heading to the airport with her forensic kit in tow. This is a little different as it's Europe, and the laws and processes vary from country to country."

"Haven't you already worked in Europe?" asked another friend.

"Yeah, we had a case that covered Belgium, the Netherlands, and Germany. We also had a recent case in Scotland although that's not part of Europe. Definitely cases outside of the United States are harder for a variety of reasons. After we're done with lunch, I'm going to research Sicily and its volcano to understand what we're walking into and what my sources might be. I'm sorry Randy's dead, but I'll admit I'm excited to tackle this case and help Brenda and Randy's family find answers."

After a few more questions, they ordered lunch and wine and caught up on each other's lives. Eventually they circled back to Marie's potential case.

"How exciting that you get to solve murders all over the world. What's your favorite part of working on one of these cases?"

"I enjoy the research, and I love that we can catch the criminal at the end."

"What's your least favorite part of these cases?"

"We've been chased down by some of the killers. That scares the wits out of me, but Jill is the one that's been targeted the most."

"Maybe it's the mafia. Isn't Sicily filled with people that belong to the mafia?"

"I don't know. Maybe that was true at one time, but even in the United States, organized crime had declined compared to what it was in the 1920's or 1930s. I guess if we take on this case, I'll find out just how powerful they are at present."

Marie had finished dining with her friends and was on her way home when Brenda called.

"Hey sis, what's going on there?"

"I'll tell you about that later, I have Randy's daughter, Melissa, in the room with me and she wants to hire your group. How does she do that?"

"Dr. Jill Quint is the leader of our group and she'll need Melissa to sign a contract. She needs the next of kin's permission to perform an autopsy. She's a forensic pathologist and licensed private investigator. She's on standby for this case. Should I have her send the contract to your email address? Do you have the ability to print, it sign it and send it back? Then it's a matter of finding a seat on a plane to Italy from San Francisco. I'm sure she's looked into possible flight times, and may be able to give you booking information by the time you send the contract back."

"You're coming too, aren't you?"

"I can do a lot of research from the states, so it's not often necessary for me to be on the scene."

"Melissa wants you all here as she feels that will help to find the murderer sooner."

"Okay, but there's a cost to that and I don't know Jo Pringle and Angela Weber's availability. In fact, I think Angela is in Italy now for the wedding of her goddaughter. She's not on the island of Sicily, but she's close by. I let you know, when and if we are all coming."

"I need you here. You know I've worked for Randy Chen for twenty years, and his death is a shock."

"Okay sis, let me see what I can do. Do you want me to email our arrangements to you or should I call you?"

"Email me, that way we don't have to worry about the time difference in terms of communicating with each other. By the way the closest airport is Catania, but if you can get here sooner by going to Palermo, then do so. The budget won't be a problem, so go ahead and book business class seats."

"Really? Are you sure? There's a section on Jill's contract where the family will specify an approximate budget and just getting us there on short notice will cost a lot."

"I'm sure, and I'll tell them to start you off with $50,000, but tell Jill to suggest an amount in her email to the daughter that will cover your initial travel, hotel fees, your daily rate, and any costs for the autopsy that she might incur."

"Okay. Let me get off the phone to call Jill and the others, and I'll see you soon."

Marie called Jill and relayed the information. An hour later, she had a signed contract and a deposit to pay for their flights. Marie contacted Jo and also confirmed with Angela's mother that she was in Italy already and her goddaughter's wedding was the previous day. She called Angela, but her call wasn't picked up, so she left the details of the case and a request to call her. Jo couldn't get off work for three days and could only stay for four days, while Marie had an entire week to give Jill. Angela might have photo engagements that she had to return to the United States for or she might have time to help on the case. She'd been taking Italian lessons and was good at learning languages so she'd be especially helpful in the investigation.

Jill emailed her flight arrangements and confirmed that

Nathan would be joining them. Marie booked her own flight and that of Jo's later in the week. Then her phone rang and she saw it was Angela.

"Hello Angela, how are you? How's was the wedding?"

"Mackenzie was a beautiful bride, and it went off without a hitch. No last minute histrionics by anyone. I saw your email, and I can head over to Sicily this afternoon. I had some side trips planned for after the wedding, but this case seems equally interesting. I distantly know our victim as he served on a couple committees at the same time as me. What a loss for his family and the community! He was highly thought of. I went to school at St. Norbert with his daughter. Is she over in Italy at the moment?"

"Yes, she's signed the contract to hire us."

"When are you and Jill arriving?"

"Tomorrow, before dinner for Jill and I arrive the next day."

"See you soon, safe travels. I'll book all of us a hotel."

"Good, Jill was hoping you would take care of that as our Italian speaking teammate."

"Ciao."

CHAPTER 2

Jill Quint, MD, made a record number of arrangements since receiving the call from Marie. She got the contract and a wire deposit from the family of Mr. Chen. She'd been able to make flight arrangements to leave that night from San Francisco. They were connecting in Istanbul to the Catania airport. With the flight arrangements made, Nathan was hustling to reschedule his clients, while Jill was making arrangements to perform an autopsy in Italy. Four hours after the initial call from Marie, they were on their way to the airport.

After buckling up their seat-belts, Jill said, "Whew! This is going to be an adventure. I've never touched the Italian justice system before, but I know from previous pathologist meetings that their autopsy system is bad."

"How so?" Nathan asked.

"They certify most violent deaths without an autopsy, and when they do an autopsy, it's wrong more than a quarter of the time, and a third of death certificates have no cause of death."

"That bad, huh? How about guns? Do they have a lot of them in Italy?"

"Don't know for sure, but I think so. The mafia is still alive and well there. I know even less about Sicily, then I do about other parts of Italy. Do you have any clients on that island?"

"Not at the moment. There are a fair number of vineyards on the slopes of Mount Etna. I met a Sicilian wine producer several years ago at a grape grower meeting, and he said to look him up if I ever visited Sicily. So I'm going to email him on the way to the airport. I don't know if he is still growing grapes or if he'll remember me. If he doesn't, there are something like five-hundred wine growers on that island, so I just may spend my time exploring them instead of meeting with clients."

"Were any of your current clients mad that you delayed meeting with them?"

"A few seemed a little put-off, but none of them has a deadline of needing a new label for a special vintage. Besides I told them I was looking for new creative ideas that might make their labels better."

"True, but you're full of creative ideas without visiting Sicily. You could probably do all of your research online."

Nathan was a world famous wine label artist and then he expanded into marketing materials for wineries, and later glass-ware and label designs for beer.

"Yeah, that's true for wine labels, but I'm interested in seeing how the wine industry advertises there. California might be the most famous wine growing region in the United States, but I bet Sicily has a harder time attracting tourists so I may see some new marketing ideas there."

"I hope I have time to visit a few vineyards that grow the Nero d'Avola grape. It's suitable for my climate and would grow well here, but it's a dry red, and my palate loves sweet white wines. So I want to sample as many bottles of that grape as possible while we're in Sicily so I can determine if I think I could have a nose for creating a great wine with that grape."

"Okay, I'll make sure to keep you supplied with that varietal of wine while we're there and maybe we can set up some wine tasting with Marie, Jo, and Angela to talk about what they like. I'll set that up once they're all there."

"Thanks, that would be perfect!"

"I'm almost afraid to ask, but what's happening to your victim's body while you're traveling to dissect him? Is he rotting in the heat?"

With a little sigh, Jill said, "That's a good question. I took a quick look at funeral homes to see if they have refrigerator coolers for their bodies and the answer is that they do. Apparently, it's an Italian tradition to kiss the face of your recently departed friend so that they don't come back to earth. Italians believe that they are helping their soul leave earth by kissing them goodbye and not speaking their name or of them. So yes they have refrigerators as no one would want to be kissing the smelly, rotting remains of Uncle Antonio."

"That's an awful picture you're painting in my mind. So they don't believe in cremation?"

"Until recently, the Catholic Church did not approve of cremation. The other factor about this case is the funeral home industry. While I was researching the mortuaries, I found an article about the mafia that was chilling. If a hospital in Sicily called an ambulance to transfer you to a nursing home, or to home to die, the mafia would pay off the ambulance attendants to inject you with air, which will cause a heart attack when the air bubble reaches your heart. Then the attendant influenced the family's choice of a funeral home by transporting dear Giuseppe's body to a particular funeral home controlled by the mafia and they would make a tidy profit on the early death."

"Sounds barbaric. Are we going to be safe in Sicily?"

"As long as the mafia isn't involved in the death of Randy Chen."

"Could they be involved?" Nathan asked, filled with trepidation over another case that could put their lives at risk.

"I haven't ruled anyone out as the source of the death. It is possible that he died of natural causes. He really could have fallen and fatally banged his head on volcanic rock," Jill said.

"Yeah right. When have you had a case recently where the person died of natural causes?" Nathan asked pessimistically seeing his tranquil Italian vacation disappearing and mafia gang members emerging from the volcanic smoke.

She just grinned over at him as they pulled into their long-term parking space at the airport. She'd insisted on them getting to the airport early as this was the first time she'd flown internationally with her autopsy case, and so she was expecting an extra round of questions coming her way. She had knives, scalpels, and flammable substances in her case along with glassware. She'd need to buy a few things in Sicily upon arrival but had already sourced them for delivery at the apartment that Angela selected. After multiple interviews on the contents of her autopsy case, Nathan and Jill were soon sitting in the relative comfort of business class for the thirteen-hour flight to Istanbul.

By the next afternoon in Sicily, Jill and Nathan were arriving at an apartment building chosen by Angela and she was aware by text of their arrival and was awaiting them outside.

"Ciao, and benvenuto a Catania," she said giving them each a hug.

"You sound like a native speaker!" Nathan said.

"Not really, I don't have much of a vocabulary, but I do believe I've nailed the Italian accent. How was your flight here?"

"Not bad. I wasn't hassled in Istanbul over the contents of my autopsy case, so I consider that a good plane ride. Did my package arrive?"

"I wouldn't want to explain why you're flying with scalpels on an airplane. You sound like a terrorist with the contents of the case, and yes a box arrived and is sitting in the apartment."

"Yeah, I suspect the U.S. Government was glad to see me go, and the Turkish and Italian security forces decided I was just too harmless. By the way, while I'm here I'm going to explore adding a new grape to my vineyard – it's the Nero d'Avola. So we're going to drink lots of that varietal here so I can determine if I think I can create a great wine with that grape. Unfortunately, we're here to do a job and I need to be at a Catania mortuary in a little less than one hour to begin Mr. Chen's autopsy."

"I'm game for the wine tasting, and how can I help on the case?" Angela asked.

"I'd like you to start by interviewing the family. What was Mr. Chen doing in Sicily? Why was he visiting Mount Etna, etc. I'm sure you know the questions to ask."

"Okay. I'll also interview Marie's sister. Should I make an appointment with the police? I assume someone took a police report."

"Actually, I didn't have time to find out if that's the case. I know they thought his death was accidental, but I'm not sure they ever completed a report. So if you can run that down, that would be great."

"It sounds like you ladies will be busy until this evening. I'm going to stock the apartment with groceries and I'll make dinner for us tonight. Drop me a text within the hour if you think of something you'd liked stocked here."

"I happen to know there's a wine store over there," Angela said, pointing across the street, "So you could start there."

"Let me drop our bags in our room, and I'll venture forth and take care of it."

Ten minutes later they had their luggage organized into one of the four bedrooms in the apartment. Nathan took a look at the cooking facilities and decided he would cook several meals for his friends and so made a shopping list.

Soon the apartment was calm and quiet as Nathan left to do his shopping. Jill and Angela sat in the living room catching up on each other's lives and the wedding. They discussed further questions to ask, and then they both left the apartment to travel to their respective locations – Mr. Chen's daughter for Angela, and the mortuary for Jill.

She was wondering if there would be anyone besides herself for this autopsy. She'd notified the consulate to notify the Italian Police before leaving California about her involvement in the case and her planned autopsy, but she suspected that she would not hear from them. Regardless she gave them the time and address for the autopsy.

Jill arrived at the mortuary to find a few cars in the mortuary parking lot. The taxi driver retrieved her autopsy case and set it on the ground for Jill to wheel into the building. One of the cars was the typical hearse, no surprise there. It was too late in the day for a funeral, and so the car would need to be parked somewhere between funerals. Two other vehicles were there, marked 'Carabinieri' and 'Polizia'. Jill hadn't known which branch of law enforcement were involved in a murder investigation in Italy as they had several forces. So she called the US Consulate General in Naples and explained her roles and responsibilities for the upcoming job in Catania.

A woman approached Jill and said in accented English, "Good day. Are you Dr. Jill Quint?"

Jill nodded and held out her hand, unsure whether Italians shook hands as a matter of business etiquette. The woman placed her hand in Jill's and said, "I'm Vice Questore Sara Cavallaro, and this is Tenete Angelo Rosso. We received a call from the United States Embassy regarding the death of Mr. Randy Chen and the fact that the family hired you to investigate Mr. Chen's death."

"Yes, I called them before I left San Francisco as I wanted to invite the appropriate Italian law enforcement representatives to this autopsy in case it provides you with any new information. Have you attended an autopsy before?"

"On rare occasion, the University of Palermo performs such an exam for the Polizia," replied Cavallaro while Rosso nodded in agreement.

"You're welcome to observe while I do Mr. Chen's autopsy."

"Why are you doing an autopsy? What are your qualifications, do you have the family's permission?" Rosso asked.

"To find the cause of death, I am a medical doctor licensed in the United States for Pathology with a sub-specialty in Toxicology, I have performed in my life probably one-thousand autopsies, and yes I have the family's permission."

"We ruled Mr. Chen's death as a non-natural death," stated Cavallaro.

"Yes, I know. I realize this is Italy, but in the United States, such an accident would require an autopsy to determine if the person fell as an accident, or was sent tumbling to their death."

"We saw no evidence of that."

"Well you wouldn't have any evidence as you didn't do an autopsy. Look, we have a different standard in the United States, and the family has hired me to carry out that standard here in Italy. Would you like to join me during the autopsy? If not, then I'll say 'ciao'."

A rapid-fire conversation in Italian followed, and beyond a few words, she had no idea what they were saying, so she turned her back on the pair to walk toward the front door of the mortuary.

CHAPTER 3

Fifteen minutes later they were all dressed in protective clothing. The mortuary staff person had declined to join Jill for the autopsy. He didn't speak English but relayed his thoughts to the two officers, and Jill was left in peace with just Mr. Chen's body and the two Italian law enforcement personnel.

She opened her kit and laid out her instruments, scale, microscope, test strips, glass tubes for blood samples, and her newest toy, a handheld ultrasound machine that could detect bone breaks and bleeds beneath her victim's skin. She started by taking blood samples that she scheduled for pick-up by a courier so that blood work could be analyzed by a forensic lab in Rome. She left that with the mortuary attendant and returned to Mr. Chen. He was a fit man in his early sixties according to his birth-date. He was five feet ten and of Asian heritage.

Holding the ultrasound, she scanned his body to see what the machine would find. She showed the two police officers what her scanner was imaging. His face had abrasions from scrapping against the volcanic rock. When Jill reached his head, she asked the two officers to assist her in turning Mr. Chen over. His skull was bloody, and her ultrasound showed a part of his cranium that was crushed, where as other parts were fracture free.

She said aloud to the two officers, "This is an unexpected finding. You would expect someone who tumbled down a steep sloop of volcanic rock to have equals fractures from the rolling effect, yet Mr. Chen's skull has just one area that is crushed. Was either of you at the scene? Are there pictures as to how he was found?"

Cavallaro pulled a folder from her shoulder purse leaning against the wall of the mortuary. She showed Jill the pictures taken of where they found Mr. Chen.

"That's odd. He was found halfway down the slope rather than at the bottom, so he didn't tumble that great a distance, perhaps ten meters and I see no rocky protuberances in the picture that might have caused the skull bashing."

The two detectives said something in Italian which Jill didn't catch, but she'd left her phone on recording the audio from the autopsy so she could make additional notes later. She'd ask Angela what they said.

Jill continued with her autopsy calling out the weights of the various organs, and other findings. She saw no signs of a heart attack or stroke that might have caused Mr. Chen to fall over the edge. She knew she needed to make arrangements for x-rays of Mr. Chen's head as that looked to her to be the cause of death. All of his other organs were simply in too great a shape to have ended his life. She wondered if the toxicology tests might show something, and she went over his skin looking for needle marks, or ligatures. His nails showed no sign of a struggle. Two hours later she finished her examination and had sewn Randy Chen back together again. She pulled her gloves off and notified the two officers that she was finished.

"Did you find a cause of death?" asked Rosso.

"Yes, and no as all of my tests are not back yet. On the surface, I would say Randy Chen died from blunt force trauma to the brain."

"So exactly as we stated on our death certificate," Cavallaro said.

"Not necessarily. In your pictures of the crime scene, I don't see what could have caused such head trauma. It is not out of the realm of possibilities that he was hit in the head with an object and then was shoved over the edge of the crater. If he had tripped or lost his balance, he would have left the rim with more speed and probably traveled further down the crater. However, if he was unconscious or even dead at the time his body was rolled over the edge, it makes sense that it would have only dropped ten meters as his body would have no momentum."

"Are you saying he was intentionally injured?" asked Rosso.

"I don't know yet, but I'm saying that the scenario is possible. Right now I need to send his body to a local radiology department to get detailed images of his brain. That will tell us if he was hit with an object in the head with an object before he was rolled over the crater edge."

Again the couple broke into Italian, and again Jill was glad she hadn't turned off her recorder as she was sure that Angela could translate for her.

"We would like copies of your report," Cavallaro said. "Perhaps we might assist you in getting the x-rays you need. Give me a moment," she said as she stepped out of the room.

Jill went to work repacking her mobile autopsy kit. The mortuary had high-level disinfectants to clean her instruments, and once she got home, she would have them sterilized for good measure. Just as she finished, the Vice Questore stepped back in the room.

"If Mr. Chen's family will agree to pay for the x-rays, then the mortuary will move his body to the hospital right now."

"They will. I don't need to go with Mr. Chen, but I would like to order a CT of Mr. Chen's skull. How do I tell the hospital to do that?"

"I took the liberty of getting a name at the hospital that's a contact person for you. Here's his name and number, and I'm told he speaks English," she said, passing a slip of paper to Jill.

Jill was a little suspicious of the process going so smoothly. Italy was known for its complicated bureaucracies.

Jill called the number and a man answered and so she started with her explanations. She was most relieved to hear that the man she was speaking with was also a physician and understood what she was asking for. After providing her billing information and where she wanted the films sent to, she ended the call. The mortuary attendant asked if she was ready to move the body to the hospital and where it was to go after that?

"As the family first directed his body to this mortuary, then I would like it returned here. I would ask that you continue to store it for the time being as I'm not ready to release it for funeral preparations."

"We weren't planning on doing anything other than storing the body. The family indicated they would make arrangement to move Mr. Chen back to his home and that they would take care of funeral preparations there."

Jill nodded and moved over to the two officers, again offering her hand for a shake.

"It was nice meeting you and I'll send you my report as soon as I have it compiled. I'm waiting on some test results that may take up to a day to receive. I'm planning on visiting the crater where Mr. Chen was found tomorrow. I'd love to meet you there to get your insight, but I understand if you're not interested or are too busy to meet me."

Again, another fast few words in Italian, then Cavallaro said, "If you give me your address, I'll pick you up at 9am and take you to the where Mr. Chen was found. Please bring sturdy hiking shoes and a coat."

"Thank you, and thanks for the reminder about my clothing, that would be perfect," Jill replied taking a moment to give her contact information to the officer.

Jill knew the two officers were watching her as she got inside a taxi after stowing her autopsy case in the taxi's trunk. As her taxi departed the mortuary, she didn't know what to make of the police. Were they interested? Were they suspicious of her or her methods, were they passive-aggressive? She wished she'd had Angela there as she was so much better at reading people. Hopefully she could take her to the crater so she could understand the two officers.

Jill returned to the apartment just after five and found Nathan creating some incredible smells in the kitchen.

"Wow, what are you making? It smells heavenly!"

"Can I tell you how much I like food shopping here? We're going to have lots of seafood and lots of pasta while we stay here. They have this fish market in the town square and you can buy any kind of fresh food. I don't think I've been this close to fresh seafood before."

Jill smiled and gave Nathan a kiss and said, "I'm so happy that you're happy shopping here. I can promise to stay out of the kitchen and give you heaps of praise for whatever you conjure up! How about wine? Did you find some Nero d'Avola samples for me?"

"Yes, and since we have some jet-lag and you don't have all of your friends here, I thought we would start with four bottles tonight. Do you know when Angela is supposed to return to the apartment?"

"I don't. She knows the daughter of this victim so her interview might take longer due to that personal connection. I'll text her and see if I get a response."

Just then they heard the apartment's front door open followed by, "Cheers, it's me and Nathan must be cooking, I could smell great food in the hallway!"

"He loves shopping for food here and cooking so all you and I have to do is eat. How awesome is that? Plus we have four bottles of wine to sample. Let have our first wine tasting after Marie arrives. Let's eat dinner and you can tell me about your interviews and I'll tell you about the autopsy. Suffice it to say, I have my suspicions about Randy's death."

"His daughter will be pleased to hear that they made a good decision bringing you in. It seems they got some grief from the local police when they showed their displeasure with their investigative skills," Angela said as they sat down to Nathan's culinary masterpiece and to discuss the four bottles of wine featuring the Nero d'Avola grape they planned on tasting once Marie arrived. Jill found herself yawning once she was replete with food.

"Oh boy, I'm going to fall asleep soon if I don't get up and move. Is there somewhere the three of us could walk and discuss our findings? Nathan, I'm assuming you want to walk with us, but if you want to stay home, I'll understand you're wanting to miss our case discussion."

"Actually, I think I'd just fall asleep if I stayed in, and I got a nice walk around Catania today so I can probably steer you towards some great places to walk."

They set forth to walk towards the large Piazza Del Duomo while they discussed the case.

CHAPTER 4

"I had two cops meet me at the mortuary," Jill started only to be cut off with "You did?!" by Nathan and Angela.

"Yes, I did. The U.S. Embassy set them on our trail, since I notified the embassy of what I was here to do."

"Did they stay for the entire autopsy? Had they seen one before?" Angela asked.

"They stayed and actually facilitated moving Mr. Chen's remains to a nearby hospital for a CT Scan and even set me up with a contact there to get the right x-rays done. So they were helpful but skeptical is how I would describe their moods."

"Were they partners? Did they speak English?" Nathan asked.

"No they came in two different cars with different police names on them. I think she represented the State Police from Palermo and he represented the Carabinieri which is the military branch of police if I understand this country's law enforcement correctly. Either they're curious or courteous because they've agreed to escort me to the crime scene tomorrow at nine."

"Do you want me to go with you?" Angela asked.

"Yes, please. I'd like you to take our own photographs of the scene, and I would be interested in your read of them. Also I had my phone on recording my comments during the autopsy so I can write my report and they spoke in Italian a few times while I was recording and I would be curious as to what they said. Let's keep quiet that you speak Italian."

"I don't speak Italian, I would say rather I understand the language better than you."

"That's more Italian than I know! I'm not sure when I'll receive a copy of the skull films from the x-ray examination, but I hope it's before we go to the site. I'm very suspicious about Mr. Chen's death as his skull was much more dented than the rest of his body. There were no defensive wounds or major scratches on his hands either."

"What do you mean defensive wounds?" Nathan asked. "What was he defending and to whom?"

"Imagine you were walking on the rim of the crater. You're looking around at the scenery and you trip on a rock that you didn't see. I mean how do you fall on the edge of the crater? You have to trip, feel faint and lose your balance, or be pushed to tumble over the edge. The edge isn't narrow and it's not like you're walking on a tightrope."

"Okay, I have your vision," Nathan said. "So if I trip, I'm going to put my hands out to try and regain my balance and save my face. If I'm pushed, again I'm going to put out my hands. If I feel faint, I might have my hands out, or I might not depending on how faint I feel."

"Yes and if you're pushed or trip you would go off the edge with some momentum, right? You wouldn't tumble just ten meters down the slope."

"So the dent in his skull and the fact he was found only ten meters below the rim makes you think he was dead weight, no pun intended, when he was pushed over the edge," Nathan said.

"That's my thinking at the moment. Of, course when we visit the crime scene tomorrow and I find a perfectly jagged rock with blood on it perhaps two to four meters below the rim, then my theory is crap."

"Has it rained here since his body was found?" asked Angela.

"I'll take some hydrogen peroxide with me which should show brown even if it has rained since his body was found. The peroxide won't tell me whether I'm looking at human or some other kind of blood, but it's a starting point. I'd also like to go down the slope, but of course I don't want to tumble to the bottom and end up dead myself."

"Will the police have some kind of climbing gear to keep you safe? Maybe I should come and Angela and I can hold a rope that's attached to you."

"The two cops can do that. While my presence may be annoying, they don't want me dead from an accident on that mountain I'm sure. I'll be sensible and I've got Angela watching my six as they say on television," Jill said with a grin. "Angela, let's hear what you found out."

"What's does that mean 'watching my six'?"

"It means I have your back and it comes from the idea that you're standing on a clock looking at '12'. Your back is facing the '6' and that's what I would be protecting."

"Okay, weird. Today I interviewed Randy Chen's daughter. She's the only one that worked for him in the family business and accompanied him on this trip. I spoke with the son by phone as well as Randy's ex-wife. As the daughter was already here in Italy and his body will return to Wisconsin for burial, the family as yet, see no reason to be in Italy."

"Why his ex-wife?" Jill asked.

"She was deeply involved in his company and was really quite distraught over his death. We can also rule out these family members as solid alibis came up in the course of our conversation. I'll interview Brenda tomorrow. In fact, since the body has been released to the family, they all may depart tomorrow with his remains back home. However we may want to keep Brenda with us as an intermediary with the family and the company. I think it would be helpful to have her onsite to answer questions rather than constantly calling or emailing her with questions. She knows our victim both personally and professionally, but I'm not sure what her role is with the company and maybe she's needed at home to manage it in his absence."

"Let's figure that out once Marie arrives, she's due to land at the airport soon," Jill said looking at her watch. "So what was Randy Chen doing in Sicily?"

"He spends a considerable amount of time outside of the United States sourcing plant substances for his homeopathic products. In fact his daughter estimated that he's out in the field as she said about half of the year. He'll explore a new product – see what people say about it, look for any evidence of the science behind the product, and then take some raw material home with him to analyze.

"He'd have his lab people study the product and decide what format to sell the product in – liquid, pill, or some other format. He'll also want to make sure he can get plenty of the product if they should go into production. Recently, the company has expanded into pet products because Americans spend so much on their pets and so why not have a cut of that market?"

"So did Melissa say what product her father was sourcing here in Sicily? I'd assume it's a plant since there are several plants that grow here and nowhere else in the world," Jill said.

"She didn't say what the exact plant was, but indicated that the leaf contained the active ingredient," Angela replied. "She said that he was super excited about the product, predicting it would become their number one product as it had multiple uses."

"Did she refuse to name the product because she didn't know or because it was a trade secret?"

"She didn't know. Her father planned to share the product with her the evening of his death, but first he wanted to 'source' it at its location somewhere on this island," Angela said signaling quote marks with her hands.

"Okay what does sourcing it mean?"

"When her father was evaluating new plant materials, he liked to go spend time with the natural product. She said he would meditate by the product as part of his decision to use something new."

"That doesn't sound very scientific," Jill commented dubiously promising herself never to order any products from her victim's company website. She remembered that she had in the past, but this idea of mediating by a new plant was just too much. Still she asked, "Did he ever reject some plants after meditating by them?"

"Let's just say, that there have been a few."

"Did Mr. Chen mention to his daughter that he would be visiting one of Mount Etna's craters? I know there are no plants up there, so that wouldn't have been his meditation location."

"She did say that he didn't mention going to the Mount Etna crater, but depending on who he ran into along the way, it wouldn't have been unusual if someone said he should go up the mountain to see the view. She did say that he often kept notes in his cellphone of what he wanted to remember about a specific plant. Melissa has his phone but can't unlock it."

"Did she have an address for where he was going to source the plant? This island is hopelessly big if we have no idea where the plant is."

"She thought he mentioned he was going to a small town with the word "Sicily" as part of the town's name. I looked up the island on a map with her on my phone and there were at least three towns with "Sicilia" in their name, but Melissa Chen wasn't really sure if that was what her father had said in passing about where he was going."

"You'll have to show me these locations on the map when we get back to the hotel. I'd like to look at them in juxtaposition to where his body was found. Did she have any clue as to what he would be using this plant material for – what ailment it would cure?"

"Her guess was weight loss as that's the outcome that so many people seek when they visit their store."

"We better head back to the apartment as Marie should arrive at any time," Nathan said as he listened to the discussion between Jill and Angela.

They turned around and started walking back to their neighborhood with Jill peppering Angela with questions, but not learning anything new about the product that Randy Chen was excited about. As they approached their apartment building they saw Marie exiting a taxi and heading to the trunk for her suitcase.

After hugs were exchanged by all, the group moved inside the building towards their rented apartment.

Once Marie placed her suitcase and backpack in one of the bedrooms, she came back to the sitting room where Nathan had a reheated dinner for her and he laid out the four wines he'd purchased earlier for them to try. Once Marie finished her dinner, Jill asked, "I understand the family is returning home tomorrow with Mr. Chen's body, do you think your sister would be willing to stay here for a few days as we try to sort out Randy and his company?"

"I don't know. She may have much to do back in Green Bay. Let me talk with her first and I'll get you an answer. How about if I invite her over to our little wine tasting party?"

"As long as she wouldn't fault us for not spending every single minute trying to solve the mystery of Randy's death."

"Not to worry. She's a Wisconsin girl, beer and wine breaks are important. Besides haven't you already done an autopsy, met with the cops and interviewed his family and you've been on Sicilian soil for what, six hours?" Marie asked.

"Yeah I guess we have been productive," Jill said with a smile. "Let's delay starting our wine testing until we know if your sister is going to join us."

A few moments later, Jill, Nathan, and Angela could tell that Brenda wasn't going to join them that night from what they heard on Marie's side of the conversation.

"She'll move in tomorrow after Melissa Chen leaves to fly back to Wisconsin. She's trying to help her at the moment. I would offer to do some work tonight, but I suspect that once we start tasting wine, I'll be falling asleep as it's been a long day getting here and I didn't sleep on the plane."

"Okay I'll admit to being a little fuzzed brained myself. I got a little sleep on the plane, but I really concentrated during the autopsy and having the two Italian cops watching my every move was different. So I'll be quick to follow you into fuzz brain-land. Is that even a word?"

"Well ladies, I've been here a few days and have no jet-lag what so ever, so I guess I'll take notes on your thoughts about the wine before you fall asleep."

"Thanks, Angela," Jill said. "Let's began our tasting!"

By the second glass of wine, Jill was beginning to yawn between swallows, by the third she was having a hard time thinking of words to describe the wine and by the forth, she was falling asleep during Angela and Nathan's conversation. He grabbed the wine glass out of her hand afraid she would spill it and steered her to bed. Marie followed at her heels.

He returned to the living room to finish the tasting with Angela. They opened the fourth bottle and took notes on the subtle flavors.

"I think this is my favorite. There are fewer aftertastes," Angela said.

"I agree. I taste fewer tannins, which means this bottle is less dry and since Jill doesn't like dry wines, I think she will like it more. We'll save some for her."

"How do you make a dry grape less dry? Didn't one of you say that the grape used for this wine is considered dry?"

"It is a dry grape, but after Jill ferments the wine she could add potassium sorbate which stabilizes the wine and prevents it from fermenting further, then she could add sugar or honey to increase the sweetness. She would probably enjoy that process and she might create a unique Nero d'Avola wine by moving away from the standard dry version."

"Sounds like a plan. How's Henrik's vineyard doing? I haven't heard much since I did the photography and you showed me the finished marketing materials."

Henrik Klein was a friend, and millionaire owner of a computer technology firm. They met him while solving his wife's murder. They had become good friends since and recently with Nathan's advice, he had purchased a winery near his home in Stuttgart, Germany. Angela did the photography while Nathan had designed the label and marketing materials.

"I chatted with him a few weeks ago and he said his first vintage was already sold out. Henrik wasn't sure if it was the wine or the label that made it so popular," Nathan said with a grin.

"He's not doing the blending himself, right?"

"No he hired a woman from California that Jill had met in her wine industry meetings. The woman had been blending in her home and produced what Jill thought were good wines and she knew she wanted to leave the competitive California market. So Henrik flew her out to the winery, interviewed her, and liked what he saw, and gave her a chance and now we've collectively helped him make his winery successful, though I'm sure he would have gotten there on his own in time. He has that magic touch."

"Yeah he was the only one to catch a thief and then marry her. He does have the magic touch. So he doesn't need us for any more work on the winery? That's too bad, I enjoyed seeing my photographs used to produce wine."

"Actually, I think you will have a lot more work coming your way if you want it. Henrik wants to do a second varietal with purchased juice since he's so impressed with his winemaker, so once he settles on the grape with her, we'll need to design materials for him. So we may need you to shoot new photographs there or locally in the United States depending on what he chooses. Also, I personally liked working with you, and I'm going to start hiring you for my own work. My current photographer is retiring, and you're top of my list to hire in the future. So if you're agreeable, I think there's a lot of travel in your future."

"Are you kidding? I loved working with you and Henrik. I knew exactly what kinds of shots to take as you painted such a clear picture in my head for Henrik's label and brochures. It was easy. Call me anytime you want."

"Good. Once this case is over, I have a job for you in Louisiana for a spirits label, and then one in Northern California for a beer label. Send me a contract that specifies your hourly rate, transportation costs, and photo editing costs, once you return home and we'll be good to go."

Angela stepped over to give Nathan a hug saying, "This sounds like brilliant fun and success in my future as a photographer. Thanks!"

"I've only worked with you on one job, but you gave me the photographs I wanted with the least amount of instruction. That's a perfect photographer for me!"

After a little more time discussing what his photography needs were in New Orleans and California, they headed off to their respective bedrooms to sleep.

CHAPTER 5

Jill, Marie, and Angela were sipping coffee in the kitchen strategizing their day. In less than an hour, Angela and Jill would accompany the two cops to the location of where Randy Chen's body was found. Jill left Nathan a note asking him about renting a car – did it make sense to rent one or to hire a driver for trying to find Mr, Chen's plant somewhere on the island of Sicily?

Marie was going to meet up with her sister as soon as Melissa left with her father's body to travel home to the United States. Jill had the x-ray films of her victim's skull and the indent looked suspicious, still Jill needed to see the crater. Melissa was glad she'd hired Jill and her team, but sad to think her father might have been murdered. Really sad as she was unaware of any enemies he had, and Melissa assumed that if the autopsy evidence proved conclusive for murder, that it was a random mugging gone bad.

Angela and Jill noted to ask the police about the personal effects found on his body. If he was carrying money or had an expensive watch on, then that negated Melissa's theory. Sicily had a high unemployment rate and was a poor region of Italy, but it wasn't known for random muggings resulting in death.

Angela spent some time listing questions for the two cops. She thought this might be the only time she got to question them. Jill made sure she had her hydrogen peroxide with her, along with gloves, q-tips, and other supplies for a forensic pathologist visiting the scene of the crime. They thought the trip to the crater would take several hours, as it, they guessed would take at least an hour to get there.

The two women were standing outside their apartment building when they saw a Polizia car approaching and Jill said, "I think that means that Vice Questore Cavallaro is driving."

The car pulled next to Jill and Tenete Rosso exited, reaching to open the back seat door of the vehicle. He paused, mid-motion noticing Angela and said, "We committed to taking you to the crime scene, not your friends."

'Okay', Jill thought. 'He's in a bad mood today. Great, just what she needed.'

"This is my teammate, Angela Weber. Her duties on the team include photography and interviewing. She's not here as a spectator. If this is a problem for you, then give me the Geo-coordinate of where Mr. Chen was found and we'll rent a car and get there on our own."

Rosso muttered a series of rapid fire Italian words and then leaned into the front seat of the car for a conversation with Cavallaro. Jill glanced over at Angela to see if she was taking it in, and she winked at Jill that she was.

Rosso returned from his conversation with his partner of the day and said, "Get in," opening the back car door for the ladies. Jill and Angela were thrilled that there were no bars separating them from the front seat, an indication that the car was not used to transport people under arrest.

Angela smiled at the two officers and said, "Buongiorno".

The two officers responded back in kind.

"About how long is the ride to reach the location where Mr. Chen was found?" Jill asked.

"It will take about forty-five minutes." Cavallaro replied.

"Who found him and called the police?" Jill asked as so far none of the details of the case had been shared with her by the family or law enforcement.

"A group of hikers approached the crater where he was found. They had halted their hike waiting for the snow to end on the mountain top around one in the afternoon. There was perhaps a two to three hour period mid-morning when no one ventured toward the crater because of light snow. We don't usually get snow in October and because it was expected to be a quick storm, the hikers waited for it to pass. Volcanic rock can be slippery when there's water on it," Cavallaro said.

"Which police force responded to the scene?" Angela asked.

"Neither of us. The hikers included a doctor who determined that Mr. Chen was dead and it looked like a tourist accident. At the scene there was no evidence of foul play as you Americans call it. An ambulance was called to remove his body, but the police were not notified until the ambulance had loaded up Mr. Chen. The hikers assisted the ambulance attendants in moving Mr. Chen out of the crater and to a stretcher. He was loaded in the ambulance and on his way back to Catania by the time Carabinieri arrived," Rosso said.

"Did you respond to the crater, Tenete Rosso?" Angela asked.

"No, one of my officers did."

"May I arrange an interview with that officer?"

Rosso looked backed at Angela with a pained expression wondering how much to cooperate with these Americans. He needed to talk with his colleagues for some input on this unusual case. Never in his fifteen year history as a member of the Carabinieri had he had an American private detective insert herself into a case. And a woman at that! The American Consulate had called his headquarters in Rome to secure their cooperation and now both he and Vice Questore Cavallaro were unsure what to do in their jobs. It was a weird and undesirable feeling.

"Perhaps."

Angela wasn't sure what to make of that answer. Was that a 'yes' or a 'no'. She decided not to push for an answer immediately as it might be a 'no', and searched for the next question to ask.

"How often are hikers injured or killed on Mount Etna?" Jill asked.

Maybe if they tag teamed the two officers, they would get more answers thought Angela.

Rosso and Cavallaro looked at each other murmuring in Italian and Rosso responded to Jill, "Neither of us remembers another death on Mount Etna, although we're sure there have been deaths and injuries when the ski lifts are operating. Also, when the volcano is active and explodes, tourists have been injured by lava exploding when it meets up with snow."

Angela shuddered at the thought of being burned by flying lava rocks and trying to move down a rocky slope away from the lava.

"Have you no warning of when the volcano is going to explode? Or are people trying to capture that on film once it has exploded?"

"Both Signorina Weber. Sometimes it's more important to capture a photograph, than to stay safe, no?"

Jill thought the Italians sure had a laid back attitude to investigating deaths at a ski resort. That would have made news in the United States, generated lawsuits, and safety inspectors would be called in to make sure other skiers were not injured or killed.

"Was there snow on the crater when your officers arrived?" Jill asked.

"No it had melted by then. As I said, this is the way with early snow. It covers the ground for less than an hour," Cavallaro said.

"So everyone's assumption was he either tripped and fell down the crater or he had a heart attack, yes?" Jill said.

"Yes," came the reply from the front seat.

"Did anyone take his temperature?" Jill asked. "Perhaps the ambulance attendants?"

"I don't know," Rosso said. "Why?"

"Randy Chen was last seen at seven in the morning according to his family, if his body was found at one in the afternoon, a core body temperature could be used to calculate his time of death. I'm also wondering if he was killed elsewhere and dumped on the crater, something I could also use the temperature for if I knew it."

There was conversation in the front seat in Italian, then Rosso began texting someone.

"We will check," he replied.

In the back seat, Angela and Jill felt like they were behaving like teenagers when she would text to Jill what was said. The two officers had a discussion about whether the case really was a murder, but Angela wasn't fluent in enough Italian to follow the entire conversation. Her conclusion was the front seat occupants thought Jill had some valid points that this death was suspicious.

"I've also requested the phone records of Mr. Chen from his family, but that may take some time to get. I thought I might be able to follow his movement on the day of his death or better still, the days leading up to his death," Jill offered.

Again the two officers nodded but didn't say anything. Jill decided they were reserving comment until they were more convinced that this was a murder investigation. Jill and Angela decided to just admire the views out the window of the police car.

They passed through small charming towns slowly heading uphill toward the top of Mount Etna. Some trees had changing leaf colors, and there was a lot of rock walls serving as fences. Eventually they climbed out of the small towns and into the start of the volcano. It was marked by copious amounts of large chunky lava rock in a dark charcoal color, and eventually a rather barren landscape. They pulled up at the base of the ski lift which was being used to ferry passengers up the mountain for hiking. There were a few patches of snow, after all Mount Etna was at nearly 11,000 feet. There was what Jill would call a snowcat parked at the end of the parking lot and Cavallaro headed over to talk to the driver as Rosso waited for Angela and Jill to exit the car carrying jackets. Jill was wearing sturdy hiking boots, while Angela had regular athletic shoes on as that was all she had packed for her trip to Italy which was only supposed to cover wedding activities. Of the two of them, Angela was much more sure-footed than Jill, and she thought they would both be okay. Jill had checked the weather on Mount Etna before she left and had packed layers for a possible trip up the mountain. As Angela was six inches taller, she had Nathan bring a jacket to keep Angela warm in case they ended up investigating Randy's death in a snow-covered landscape.

They walked over to the vehicle, which had a high suspension and massive tires. It reminded Jill of the monster truck from her previous case in Louisiana. Fortunately, there were stairs to reach the cabin. She asked the driver before she entered, "Do passengers get car sick on this road?"

Apparently the driver didn't speak English as there was a quick conversation between the two officers and the driver before Rosso said, "Some passengers have felt sick as the truck climbs over some rough terrain."

"Then, can I sit in the front seat? I do better with nausea if I sit there," asked Jill.

More conversation in Italian and then the driver escorted Jill to the front seat. Jill had read-up on the mountain and her understanding was that this vehicle would take her to a point, then they would have to hike the last bit. Based on pictures posted on the internet, it didn't look like a far walk, only one at a higher altitude than she was used to. How hard would it be to hike carrying the dead weight of a murdered man?

"Can anyone drive an off-road vehicle up this mountain or will park rangers or the polizia stop such a thing?"

"Cosa?"

Jill assumed that was the Italian word for 'what?'

"I was wondering if Mr. Chen was killed elsewhere and moved to the crater to make it look like an accident, how would you get a body up there? It would seem that you would need a car like the one we're riding in. So where would our killer get such a ride?"

"Before you think of ways to get a body up the mountain, shouldn't you have proof that Mr. Chen was murdered?" Cavallaro said.

"Unless we find something unusual on this mountain, I believe Mr. Chen was murdered," replied Jill. "That indentation of his skull is not the usual traumatic blow you see in a fall. His head should have had skull fractures throughout if he had taken a tumble. His, did not."

"Maybe you are trying to earn your consultant's fee," muttered Rosso.

"And maybe the two of you should have my expertise by having performed over one-thousand autopsies for crime labs. How many have you even watched? One, I believe you said? You have no expertise in this area," Jill said losing her temper.

There was dead silence in the van other than a little Italian muttering coming from the back. They hit rough patches in the mountain and Jill was suddenly focused on holding on to her stomach contents. With single-minded focus, she looked through the windshield at the top of the road keeping a straight horizon in her view. She was relieved when they came to a stop at the base of a slope that Jill presumed belonged to the southeast crater of Mount Etna. She was thrilled to step onto firm ground while her stomach settled. She zipped up her jacket and reached in for her backpack.

Once they all met at the front of the vehicle, Jill pointed and asked, "Is that the crater where Mr. Chen was found?"

Cavallaro opened a file she was holding and said, "Yes."

Jill proceeded up the hill knowing Angela would follow her

and not really caring whether her two police representatives did. She hadn't been aware until their conversation in the vehicle that they were not treating Mr. Chen's death as a potential murder. Note to self, if she ever wanted to murder someone, do it in Italy given their investigative skills.

The slope consisted of charcoal gray sandy dirt scattered with clusters of lava rock. Jill imagined that this was what the surface of the moon looked like although Sicily looked much more alive than any picture of the moon. They were nearing the top when she felt the ground move beneath her.

"Earthquake! If I were at home, I would tune in to the internet to find the magnitude. That felt like a 3.0 to 3.2!" Jill said to Angela.

"Let's hurry up and get off this crater! Aren't earthquakes a precursor to volcanoes blowing up?"

"Yes and no," Jill explained as she continued to the top. "The latest I read on the topic goes like this – Imagine that you're driving a truck and the bed is filled with say heavy jello and you brake. The jello will roll within the truck bed. With earthquakes, if the earth's plates move, it sloshes around the hot lava beneath us and that may cause a build-up of pressure that blows the volcano."

"I get your explanation and so shouldn't we leave? Now!"

"No. First we don't know where the epicenter of the quake was – maybe it wasn't underneath us and Mount Etna averages ten quakes a day, most too small a magnitude for us to feel. So an earthquake isn't necessarily a reason to run," Jill said with a smile as she continued her journey up.

"Yes, but what if you fall into the crater because you're shaken off your feet? And what about Pompeii. Didn't they all die shortly after a big quake?"

"I'm not worried and I'm far more likely to do myself damage by tripping. As for Pompeii, they had a big quake months before the volcano blew and their people were buried in ash. I think our monster truck can get us off the mountain before we're covered in ash."

They reached the top of the crater and looked down. Jill's immediate thought was Mr. Chen couldn't have died here in a fall. Then she questioned herself, was she being objective or was she so mad with Rosso's comment that she was jumping to conclusions. She thought back to the picture she'd seen of Mr. Chen and began searching for rocks that might have done the damage to his skull that she saw on the x-ray film.

All she saw was rocks that could have done the damage. There were hundreds of rocks of the approximate size that could have dented Mr. Chen's skull.

She looked back at Rosso and Cavallaro and asked, "May I see the photo of Mr. Chen again?"

Without a word, Cavallaro held out the photo. Angela took a picture of it between taking pictures of the crater. Jill studied the picture and then the crater going back and forth repeatedly. She moved to an area that she thought Mr. Chen was found and looked for other marks on the slope that she might be right. From the report from the two officers, there should be a sliding mark where his body slid and then a lot of footprints as people attended him. She took her hydrogen peroxide out of her backpack prepared to drop it on the rocks close to where Randy had been found.

"Scusami?" Rocco asked looking at Jill's bottle.

"I'm looking for the rock that Mr. Chen banged his head on. By pouring peroxide on these rocks, I'm looking for them to bubble up brown as evidence of iron in the hemoglobin in the blood. That doesn't begin to tell me if the blood is human or animal or indeed Mr. Chen's, but if none of the rocks bubble, then how did he get the dent in his skull?"

Jill studied the slope which wasn't as steep as she feared and she had good traction from her hiking boots. She gingerly stepped down the slope sprinkling the various rocks with her peroxide.

The only rocks that bubbled were too small to cause the damage Jill saw in Mr. Chen's skull. Still Angela took a bunch of photos and Jill collected the rocks that bubbled with iron. Mr. Chen had bled from the back of his skull and so she could check to see if the blood on the rock matched her victim's. That really didn't tell her anything new, but it might be useful later.

She stood on the slope and looked up at Tenete Rocco and Vice Questore Cavallaro and asked, "Do you officers see a rock that made the dent in Mr. Chen's head? Have I missed something?"

"What size rock are you looking for?" asked Cavallaro.

"It needs to be at least fifteen centimeters."

The two officers looked around and then Jill felt the ground shifting underneath her again as another earthquake hit the area. Before she knew it, she was sliding down the crater, and when she came to a halt, she was now one-hundred feet below the rim of the crater. Her hands were scratched and she was dusty, but otherwise, the no worse for wear. She stood up and waved to Angela and the two officers signaling that she was fine. She studied the slope and decided if she moved about fifteen feet to the right, the pitch of the slope would be less and so she thought she had a better chance of climbing out of the crater. She set out on the climb and was soon short of breath given the altitude of nearly ten-thousand feet, but she really wanted off the mountain before another earthquake hit.

Upon reaching the top and short of breath, she said between gasps, "Let's get out of here! I'm done."

"Are you hurt?" Angela asked.

"My hands took a beating," Jill said holding out her scratched and bleeding hands. "I think that the last earthquake proved a point. I believe Mr. Chen was dead when his body was disposed of in the crater. Why else would his hands lack scratches like these from the lava rock," Jill said holding out her hands. "I know from his autopsy that he didn't have a heart attack or stroke. He had no history of diabetes. I have no medical reason for him to black-out so quickly that he didn't have time to put his hands out before he fell to the ground. I think he was placed in the crater in the position he was found."

Jill said these last words looking at Rosso and Cavallaro who had said nothing to this point.

Finally Cavallaro spoke up and said, "You have some very good points Dr. Quint. I think we must contact our prosecutor and open this case as a potential murder investigation. I will need you, your autopsy results, and any test results you get back to be made available to our prosecutor. I will try to arrange an interview immediately. When are you planning to leave Sicily to return home?"

"I would guess I will be here for at least a week. The family has engaged me to investigate Mr. Chen's death and to proceed with an investigation of my own if I find he died under suspicious circumstances. The results of the autopsy yesterday and my inspection of the site today have caused me to conclude that our victim has died under very suspicious conditions."

Within the hour, Jill and Angela had returned to their apartment in Catania just as Marie and her sister were arriving by taxi. Cavallaro and Rocco had driven away with Jill's contact information and the admonishment to stay available for their prosecutor.

CHAPTER 6

Jill had met Brenda before, but it had been several years. She held out her hand and said, "Sorry for your loss. I'm fairly convinced and I've almost convinced the Italian police that Mr. Chen was murdered."

Brenda knew from what Marie had said that this was the likely conclusion that Jill was heading toward, but the words soon had tears pouring out of her eyes, "That's so sad. He was so full of life and good ideas and he was loved by his family."

Brenda found herself in a group hug by everyone. Angela dug out a tissue and when she had a moment of composure she asked, "Have you notified Melissa?"

"No. Do you know if she has internet access? I'm not sure where she is at the moment."

Brenda finished wiping her tears, looked at her watch and thought about what Melissa said was her schedule.

"She's en route to Rome or she may have landed there. She has a long journey home with Randy's remains. The fastest route included connections in Rome, then Atlanta, and then home to Green Bay."

"Okay, thanks. I'm going to go upstairs and make the call to her cell phone from the apartment and see if I can reach her. It sounds like if she isn't available now, she will be in a few moments."

The apartment building had a small elevator, so Jill and Angela took the stairs while Marie and Brenda and her luggage followed in the elevator with all of them arriving at the same time. Marie was showing Brenda into the room they would share, while Jill went into her bedroom to make the call. Nathan had left a note that he was out at a cafe for breakfast and to call him if she needed him.

Jill took a moment to write a few notes down of what she wanted to convey to Melissa Chen, then she dialed her cell phone.

"Hello?"

"Hi Ms. Chen, this is Dr. Jill Quint and I wanted to provide you an update. Is this a good time?"

"Yes, I just exited one plane and my next is set to board in ninety minutes. What have you found?"

"I'm afraid that I'm reaching the conclusion that your father did not die of natural causes. I don't have a confirmation on that yet, but I expect I will by this time tomorrow."

"Oh, God."

Jill waited a few seconds trying to judge what was happening on the other end of the line. Had Melissa fainted, or did she want to say more?

"Ms. Chen?"

"Yes, I'm here," said a shaky voice.

Jill hated giving this kind of news over the phone, but she had no choice. Melissa needed to escort her father's remains home and plan a funeral. Jill gave her the details of what they had seen at the crater that morning, the earthquakes, and the entry of the Italian police into the case.

"I don't have your father's toxicology results back yet. I had them flown to a Swiss Lab known for its accuracy. It will take longer, but I'll feel more confident with the results."

"Okay," was all Melissa Chen said.

"At this point, you could save your family money and end my services and let the Italian Police take-over."

"Are you kidding? Let them take over the investigation? I have no faith that they will get it correct," Jill heard the strength return to Melissa's voice with these comments. "Use your PI license and find my father's killer!"

"Alright then, I always want to check in with the family to see if they still want me on the case as it will save you money."

"Spend whatever you need to find my father's killer and I mean that. If he were here, that's what he would say."

"Okay. I should have an update for you once you arrive in Atlanta that I'll provide by email. Call me anytime. I know the Italian police will ask for this and I would like it first, but could you mail me your father's cellphone from the airport now with his password if you have it?"

Jill knew the cellphone had been with Mr. Chen at the time of his death as she had asked Melissa what personal effects the police had turned over to her.

"I'll find a way to get it to you before I leave Rome, but I don't have his password."

"That's okay. I know someone in the security business in Germany that's really good with breaking phone passwords."

"Wait a minute, Dad may have trade secrets on his cell phone, I don't want it outside of your hands."

"Not to worry, the last phone my friend unlocked, he did so in front of me and handed the phone over without examining it. It's my intent to examine the last few days to see if I can determine where your father went and who he met with. Based on what I saw at the crater, I believe this to be a well-organized murder."

"I don't understand."

"I don't believe your father to be a random victim of violence. Someone had to have a special vehicle to get your father to the crater as I saw no evidence that he was killed there. I believe he was killed elsewhere and his body moved to the crater to make it look like an accident. Certainly it fooled the Italian police."

"Oh," Melissa said and then after a pause added, "Would it help if I got information from his phone provider on where he used the phone recently?"

"Exactly what I am looking for. In addition to any emails or texts that might indicate a meeting location, your father's phone should have pinged looking for towers everywhere. That might help pinpoint where he was when he met his killer."

"I have a friend that works for a telephone company at home. I'll call her to see how I can go about getting that information for you."

"Great. I know you have a funeral to plan, and it's rude of me to ask, but that telephone information is central to this investigation. The Italian police may be able to access it sooner than I, but I'm not sure of Italian laws in regards to obtaining that kind of information. I would also expect them to call you for an interview."

"Okay. Should I tell them you have his phone?"

"Let me think about that question. I don't like lying to the police, but I'm also not convinced that they might screw up the phone somehow. I'll leave you an email answer by the time you land in Atlanta. On second thought, I'll have my friend unlock the phone and I'll copy its contents, then give it to them locked. I bet they don't have a resource to unlock the phone."

"I like that answer Dr Quint. I'm worried given the history of Sicily, that the mafia or someone else might have bought off the police. I don't know if that's an old rumor, or if it's how it is today, but at least if we have a copy we have proof if they destroy some part of it. I'll make sure I don't return the call until I have an email from you saying your expert has managed to unlock and copy the phone for you."

"Do you have any other questions, Melissa?"

"I'm sure I do, but none I can think of at the moment. I need to get moving on arranging this phone be sent to you in Catania. You've made me suspicious, so I'm going to have the package held at the airport in Catania requiring you and your passport to pick it up if that's okay."

"Yes that's fine. I'd tell the airline agent that you just left your twenty-year-old daughter to travel by herself and walked off with her phone and it's a parental emergency to get it back to her. You can say that I'm your daughter's aunt and she'll be returning to stay with me after she does an all-day hike up the volcano - both you and her are in a panic with her not having the phone."

"Thanks Jill, that's a great cover story that I'll have no problem acting out. Again thanks for your help and I'll go handle getting this phone delivered to you and text you the pick-up information."

Jill ended the call and returned to the apartment's living room to discuss with her team and Brenda. Nathan was still out and about which was fine. Jill was glad he was enjoying himself in the city of Catania.

"Did you reach Melissa?" Brenda asked.

"Yes I did and we had a lengthy conversation about Mr. Chen's phone. She has it with her, but she's making arrangements to have it flown back to the Catania airport this afternoon. Then I think I'll need Henrik's niece to come and unlock it before I hand it over to the Italian police.

"Who's Henrik?"

"Someone that we hope Marie dates someday," Angela said with a smile. "He's a former client and special man who helps us with security type questions on our cases occasionally. He's the guy we visit whenever we head off to Germany. In a previous case in Wales and Scotland when our good friend Nick was murdered, he sent his niece to us and she unlocked the phone in about five seconds. So Marie, go call Henrik and see if we can have his niece here this afternoon or evening."

Jill grinned at Angela's machinations while Marie rolled her eyes as she left the room to make the call and Brenda said, "What?"

"We think Henrik is a super-nice widower. It's been over two years since we solved his wife's murder and Angela, Jo, and I think Henrik would make a great match for Marie. The biggest problem seems to be that he's in Germany and she's in Wisconsin, but he has a private jet and a personal fortune and so they could make dating work. We'll have to see what happens."

"I didn't know that about my sister or really understand the work that the four of you do. I'm impressed and glad I mentioned to Melissa that you could help."

Marie came back into the living room with a grin on her face and this time it was Jill who said, "What?"

"Henrik's going to come to the apartment tonight for dinner. I volunteered Nathan to cook for all of us. It's just a two-hour journey in his plane and so he expects to be here about six. He says he can crack the phone. I hope he's as good as his niece was."

"Let me call Nathan so he can plan dinner and get some wine. This will be a great evening!" Jill said. "Then I need to get back to the case. I'm going to check to see if any lab results are in and then Brenda, I'd like to chat with you on whatever new product Mr. Chen was working on or excited about. We don't have any clue what the motive is for his murder other than it likely wasn't random. It could be personal with someone mad at him for something – perhaps in his personal life or even a deranged employee. The motive could also be business if he was about to land a new multi-million dollar miracle product that someone else wanted."

"Wow, when you put it like that, it feels like you're looking for a needle in a haystack. Randy has touched so many people and now they're all suspects," said Brenda.

"Actually most of them could probably prove they weren't in Sicily at the time of his death, but you can always hire someone to do the dirty deed. So only people with the means to pay for an assassination would stay on my list of suspects."

"How much does murder for hire cost?" Brenda asked, then seemingly appalled by her own question she added, "Oh my God, I can't believe I just asked that question."

"It's okay. It's one we would ask ourselves as a means to eliminate suspects. Sicily has high unemployment so I would guess that it would be cheaper to hire a killer here than in the states. That said, Mr. Chan's body was moved to the crater and that might be a costly expense depending on what vehicle was used and whose silence had to be bought. Frankly it sounds a little more sophisticated than the average street thug might plan."

Angela and Marie were nodding with Jill words, then Marie said, "Let's follow up on the idea that Randy had a meeting somewhere in a town with the word Sicily in its name. I'll check the cities – see what I can find about them and if they have an unusual or abundant plant that grows in that area."

Brenda asked her sister, "Can I help? Give me something to research and I'll do my share."

Jill smiled and said, "Thanks, Brenda, for helping Marie. I'd also like to look into this new product Mr. Chen was sourcing. Can you think back through conversations or emails with him and recall any obscure comments that might direct us toward identifying whatever this new product was?

"I'm going to check into getting a car rental. Since I need to return to the airport to get Melissa's package, I may as well pick up a car at the same time. I think we're going to end up traveling around the cities at the base of Mount Etna. I hear driving here is insane, who wants to be the driver?"

"How about we designate Nathan? He did a good job in Scotland on the wrong side of the road," Angela suggested.

"I like that idea as he has more experience driving in Europe because of his business trips here. Angela, can you skim through my taping of the autopsy to see if the two cops said anything important there?"

"Si," Angela said in her best Italian accent.

Nathan walked in just as everyone was hunkering down with their assignments. He leaned in to kiss Jill and said, "Got your text, so I've been volunteered to cook for all of you and Henrik! That'll be fun. I'm going to check a few recipes, then I'll head out to the store."

"Ah, babe, I need something else from you first. I need to go to the airport in about an hour to pick up a package from Melissa Chen and while there I want to rent a car for you to drive. I'm too scared to drive here."

"Really? You're a terror on the roads in California. You don't want to take on the drivers here?" he said with a grin.

"Nope!"

Nathan took a quick look at the time, did some calculation and said, "I can manage to shop and get the rental car. Let me just figure out where to park around here."

Angela looked up and said, "I could go outside now and talk to the neighbors and see what they say about parking. Then I'll listen to your autopsy tape."

Later that afternoon, each of them had something new to add to the butcher paper on Randy Chen that was taped to the living room wall. It was the easiest way to keep everyone informed and Jill always packed it in her traveling autopsy suitcase.

Hours later, the car was parked on a nearby street. Henrik arrived and unlocked Randy Chen's phone, and now they were gathered around the apartment table drinking wine and talking about the wine industry.

"It's nice that you frequently need my help on these cases near to my home. What will you do if your next case is in the United States?" Henrik asked.

"We'll figure out some way to get your help long-distance. You might have to teach us all to be phone hackers as that appears to be an ongoing skill we need," Jill said cheerfully.

"Or you could come to the U.S. more frequently," Marie added.

"I enjoy your company, my friends, and so if I can work it into my schedule, I'll drop in on you the next time you need help."

"We'll be in Eastern Canada for our next vacation if you would like to join us. We'll be exploring Ice Wine which is also suitable for your part of Germany. When was the last time you took a vacation?" Jill asked.

"It's been a long time. I'll think about it," was all Henrik would say.

The conversation moved on to other topics, and then Henrik had to head back to the airport for his flight home. Marie walked him out to his taxi, while the friends returned to the case.

CHAPTER 7

Jill was up the next morning with many to-do items on her list. First she needed to check on her test results, that was to be followed by emailing Melissa Chen, and reviewing Randy Chen's unlocked phone as Henrik had been successful in unlocking the password. She took her laptop into the living room so that Nathan could sleep in peace. She hoped by the time he woke up that she would have a few places to visit where Mr. Chen might have been on the day of his death.

Marie also an early riser, looked up from her laptop and said, "Good morning, did you sleep well?"

"How could I not between the jet lag and the fabulous evening. It was wonderful spending some time with Henrik."

"Yeah, he's a great man. It's kind of scary to watch him unlock a phone. I have so many items in my contacts app that I wouldn't want just any hacker to get their hands on."

"Yeah I know what you mean. Fortunately, my cell phone company has great security and if I'm ever murdered, I'd want Henrik to unlock my phone to help find my killer and that's what we're doing."

"True."

"So do you think you two will ever date?"

"I don't know. I find him attractive and nice. He brought me my favorite chocolate from Germany, but I'm not sure he's over the death of Laura. There's this lingering sadness every once in a blue moon that makes me think he's thinking of her."

"I know what you mean. It's faint, but I catch it too once in a while - like he wishes she was there to enjoy our company, but then he seems to shake himself out of it. From what he said of her, I doubt we would have been friends or if we would have socialized with her as she had this dark side to her."

"Yeah I try to avoid folks on the dark side. They're never worth the drama about them and if I could ever develop an accurate screening tool, I would never hire one of them as they inevitably cause some workplace problem. So not to change the topic, but Brenda wrote some thoughts and I have a few cities for us to visit, but I think from what you said yesterday, you have a few priorities to take care of before you get to me."

"I've been looking at the toxicology screen results while we were chatting and I see the proof that Randy was murdered. Melissa will be relieved to know that he was likely unconscious when he was thumped on the head."

"How can you tell?" Marie asked, pausing in her own computer search.

"His lab results came back with Chloroform in his blood and tissues. Chloroform used to be an anesthetic before better compounds were created. It's toxic to the kidney and liver and disappears quickly. So he must have died soon after he was administered the drug, as his kidneys and liver didn't have time to work it out of his system. That's a mistake on the part of the killers, perhaps if they waited twenty minutes after knocking him out, it would have dissipated and we would have never known."

"I rather like the thought that he was unconscious when someone took a big rock to his skull."

"Yes, I would rather be anesthetized for that."

"Is it hard to get chloroform in Sicily?"

"I don't know. I need to send Melissa Chen this information and then notify our police contacts. Let me handle those tasks and then we'll move on to your stuff," Jill said adding the latest information to her wall poster on the case.

Jill took one more look at the toxicology tests to see if anything else was abnormal. She wasn't surprised to see Randy's liver had reacted to the substance as that was one of the toxic problems of chloroform. Then with some thought she composed an email to Melissa. She also read the report on the rocks she collected in the crater and the blood on them wasn't human. It would be faster to just relay the results, but she needed to add some empathy and explanation. It took a while, but eventually she was satisfied with her wording. She hit send, then looked over to Marie and said, "Tell me what you learned."

"There are eight cities with some form of the word Sicily in their name. Some are close to Mount Etna and others are much closer to Palermo. Their websites, once translated to English, talk about wonderful flora and fauna along with lots of ancient churches and ruins. The towns range in size from 500 people to ten thousand. Several towns have olive oil festivals and others have hazelnuts, lots of wine varietals, and prickly pears."

"So your search is still too wide at the moment. Did Brenda remember anything that was helpful?"

"Yes, she did, our minds must think alike. She thought back over the past three months about conversations with Randy. She remembers in a meeting that he spoke of a couple of plants that were on his radar for new products. She couldn't remember when the meetings were if he said where he had sourced the plants. He listed several, but she could only remember two – Aloe Vera and Hippocrates' tree."

"The Plane-tree, platanus oreintalis in Latin."

"I forget about your botany background. I'm amazed you can remember Latin names so easily."

"It's one of the few names I remember because of its connection to Hippocrates. I don't think I could have named a single plant we saw on the slopes of Mount Etna yesterday. So are both plants here? If I recall they like the Mediterranean climate and would do well in areas of Sicily where it doesn't freeze."

"Yes, that's what my research showed. One of the cities on my list gets snow, so I think we can cross that one off."

"I agree with the snow. I'm not aware of anything special about Aloe Vera or Plane-tree in Sicily. These are not rare plants and they grow in many areas of the world. Why would Randy Chen think he could only source the plants here? And these are two common plants, who would kill over them?"

"I don't know. We seem to have more questions than answers," said Marie.

"Let me get to work on Randy's phone to see if there's anything there that will help us pinpoint Randy's travels and product development. I would think that sometime today, the Italian prosecutor will reach out to us. I'm rather surprised that it didn't happen yesterday."

"Yeah I find that weird also, but then I think I've really learned in this case, how important the work of a medical examiner's autopsy is in determining the cause of death. If the family hadn't hired you, no one would have recognized this as a murder."

"I briefly did some research before arriving and was appalled at how they handle autopsies. Overall, Italy is considered to have a low murder rate, but if they miss classifying deaths as murders as they did in this case, then that statistic may be considerably inaccurate for this country."

"Good morning!" Angela said coming into the living room and sitting down. "What new clues have you discovered at this hour of the day?"

"Good morning yourself!" Jill replied. "I have one new clue - there was chloroform in Randy's blood that caused a little liver damage. And that indicates he was definitively murdered."

"How sad," Angela said pausing and thinking about Randy's reputation in her community and his daughter Melissa. "What do the police say about that? They seemed so hesitant yesterday to declare his death a potential murder. Mother Nature had to throw two earthquakes at them to get her point across."

"Two earthquakes? I don't recall hearing about that," Marie said.

"Yeah, it was divine providence. We were walking up the slope to the crater and an earthquake hit which rather freaked me out. Jill here, our resident volcanologist, assured me we wouldn't soon be covered in dust and suffocate like Pompeii. So perhaps twenty minutes later, while she was on the inside slope of the crater sprinkling rocks looking for blood, a second earthquake hit that caused her to slide down the slope. She quickly regained her traction and rushed to the top before a third quake hit, but her hands were scraped in the slide and the cops agreed that as Mr. Chen had no defensive wounds on his hands, it was unlikely that he'd had an accident causing him to fall into the crater."

"Wow! How are your hands this morning? What an adventure!"

Jill held her palms up and they could see some scratches on the palm, but it didn't look bad.

"My hands are fine, and yes I don't know what to call it other than divine providence when the quake hit and it served to make my point. As to what the police say, I haven't told them yet. I emailed Melissa first, then I wanted to hear what Marie had found yesterday, and now I'm composing an email to Tenete Rosso and Vice Questore Cavallaro. I don't know what time they start work in Sicily, but I would expect to hear from them shortly after they open the email. Depending on their criminal justice procedures in Italy, they may need to follow the body to the United States and get additional blood samples and send it to a police lab there or here so they have the results for a trial. My technique didn't follow the rules of evidence custody."

"Can they do that? Test after a person has been dead for several days? Doesn't it dissipate?"

"No, we could dig Randy Chen back out of the ground a year from now and we would find the chloroform in his liver. I informed Melissa to wait on letting anyone prepare Randy's body for burial as the Italian Police might request further testing. I expect an answer today, so this shouldn't delay things too much."

Angela looked sad at the thought of digging Randy out of the ground a year after his death, while Marie looked grimly fascinated.

"It seems like I've heard of some famous people being exhumed and tested to see what killed them – like prior kings or something."

"Yes, one recent case was Simon Bolivar, the revolutionary from Venezuela. The ex-President, Hugo Chavez had him dug up seeking to prove he died by arsenic poisoning rather than tuberculosis. The autopsy was inconclusive, but I don't remember who conducted it to tell me if I would have trusted their methods, but there have been a variety of famous people exhumed."

Jill's cell phone rang and she noted that Melissa was calling. She must be between planes in Atlanta. She had a short conversation with her explaining where she was with the case and next steps. She no sooner ended the call with Melissa than she noted an Italian phone number was calling. She wondered if this was Rosso or Cavallaro, or perhaps they had robot-callers in this part of the world too.

"Hello."

"Is this Dr. Jill Quint?" asked an Italian accented voice?

"Yes."

"This is Pubblico Ministero Lombardo. I have Tenete Rosso and Vice Questore Cavallaro here with me. Are you familiar with the Italian justice system Dr. Quint?"

"I looked it up before leaving for Italy so I have a vague idea. I believe that when officers have some evidence of a crime that needs further investigation, a prosecutor enters the case to direct the investigation. I believe that must be you. Is that correct?"

"Yes, that's a nice summary. I visited the location where the American Mr. Randy Chen was found by hikers four days ago. After discussing the case with my associates I agreed there were enough unexplained circumstances to Mr. Chen's death. As I was meeting this morning with Tenete Rosso and Vice Questore Cavallaro, they received the communication from you that Chloroform was recorded in his blood. Is that correct?"

Jill had placed her phone on speaker mode and now Marie and Angela were sitting in silence following the conversation.

"Yes, that's correct. As a forensic pathologist, I can tell you that there's no medical reason for that substance to be in his blood other than for him to have inhaled it. If he voluntarily inhaled it, we would have found evidence of a bottle of chloroform near him along with a cloth, as he would immediately crumple to the ground within a few inhalations. According to the first responders, this was not the case. So at this point, I would conclude that Mr. Chen involuntarily inhaled the anesthetic."

"I see, Dr. Quint. Can you tell me where Mr. Chen's remains are at this time? I am sure I can contact the family, but I would like to avoid unnecessary contact at this time of grieving for them."

"I spoke with the daughter just a few minutes ago as she was changing planes in Atlanta in the United States. I asked her to avoid making any funeral preparations for twenty-four hours as the Italian police might want to collect forensic evidence that demonstrated a chain of custody. I can give you the contact information for the Green Bay Police so that you can arrange official evidence collection once his remains land there in a few hours."

"Forgive my ignorance, but the chloroform will have disappeared from his blood after this length of time, no?"

"Actually, you could collect the blood sample a year from now and it would still be there. Also, you can't inject or put a cloth over his face after his death and have it show up on testing. Without his lungs breathing and blood circulating it won't travel inside his body. His liver shows signs of damage from the chloroform and again that damage occurred while he was still alive."

"Yes, do you have any advice on the tool that was used to dent his head?"

"Let me examine the CT results. I may be able to give you a description of the surface of the item that he was hit with as well as the possible angle of the person holding the weapon. I can tell you it was not a sharp instrument like a knife."

"I would like to share your results with our doctor for analysis. May we have a copy of your report?"

"I shared with your officers the autopsy report and some of the lab work. I will send you the CT scan and report as well as any further lab results I receive from my Swiss lab. Do you have a forensic pathologist in Sicily to interpret the results for you?"

Jill heard an exhale on the other end of the phone line and then Pubblico Ministero Lombardo said, "The University of Catania has a Forensic Medicine division that I will contact to act on our behalf. Would it be possible to arrange a meeting with them, yourself, and my office today, Dr. Quint?"

Jill thought about what she was planning to do. Her first allegiance was to Melissa Chen and so she wanted time to review Randy's cellphone. It was still mid-morning.

"Yes and I'll bring my team with me. How about at two this afternoon? If you'll give me an address, we'll make our way there. The University is a few blocks from our apartment and we would enjoy the walk."

"Your team?" she heard the prosecutor ask and there was conversation in Italian in the background. Then he came back on the line and said, "Ah, my colleagues have informed me about your team. Then we shall see you later."

The call ended and Jill felt a minor rumble beneath her feet.

Marie looked up in alarm and so she and Angela said simultaneously, "Earthquake."

"What should we do?" asked Marie.

"On the case or for the earthquake?" Jill replied.

"The earthquake! Shouldn't we do something?"

"That felt like a 2.5 on the Richter scale to me, or it was far away. So we do nothing. If the quake feels stronger run for any doorway or if you're outside, stay away from building and power wires as they may come tumbling down. Doorways are supposed to be reinforced, but I can't vouch for the same construction standards in Sicily."

"Is the volcano about to blow? Should we worry about breathing ash or getting a flight out of here?"

Again Angela and Jill said, "no", at the same time and then smiled at each other. Jill gestured to Angela to explain.

"There are many earthquakes on the island of Sicily, but not all of them are related to volcanic activity. Some of the most deadly eruptions of Mount Etna happen without an earthquake or an earthquake that occurred many months before the eruption, so we will be long gone before we need to worry about the volcano erupting from an earthquake."

"The thing with earthquakes is you need to know the magnitude and epicenter to determine your level of damage. There was a bad earthquake in Messina which is the closest point to where Sicily meets the mainland. The cause of that quake was the plate in the strait of Messina. It had nothing to do with Mount Etna. So what we're telling you is you're in a region that is prone to earthquakes. You can't predict them, rather you just need to know what precautions to take when they happen. Okay?"

"I guess you're telling me there's nothing we can do about the quakes other than to leave the island, or maybe I should say get out of Italy since I think I've heard of bad quakes on the mainland as well."

"Yes that's a good summary," then seeing Brenda approaching

the living room, she said, "Good morning Brenda, did you sleep well?"

"Yeah, I did for the first time since Randy's death. As weird as this sounds, I feel better about his murder because at least I didn't fail to notice that he was in poor health, which is what I first thought. You don't just die of a heart attack, you have symptoms and I feared I hadn't noticed them. Then I worried about all of the additives that Randy took and maybe one of his additives caused his own early death."

Jill, Angela, and Marie gave a Brenda faint smiles. They understood what she was saying and acknowledged that it was weird.

"So any new information this morning?" Brenda asked.

"Yes, actually a lot of changes overnight," Jill replied. "I received some of the blood work back and Randy Chen had chloroform in his blood which is proof that he was murdered as there was no evidence that he voluntarily inhaled it. Also the Italian prosecutor called and we have a meeting this afternoon with him and his team at the University of Catania Forensic Department. Melissa Chen has changed planes in Atlanta, and the prosecutor will be contacting the Green Bay Police to assist with getting forensic evidence from Mr. Chen's body once it arrives there. I lack the appropriate credential to do the chain of evidence on his blood work.."

"Wow, that is a lot of new information overnight. So Randy somehow inhaled chloroform and then once he was unconscious he had a deadly blow to the head. So how did he end up in the crater and who killed him and why?"

"That's the amazing part of these cases. On the one hand you feel like you make these giant leaps forward with new information. But then you ask yourself – why is the person dead and who killed him or her and then it feels like you're back at square one," Marie said.

"We do have a giant leap in that we have essentially proved that he was murdered and the Italian police have entered the investigation," Jill said. "Now we need to examine his phone to see if there are any clues therein."

"Are we going to mention the phone to the Italian prosecutor?" Marie asked.

"Yes, though I haven't told them about it yet. We have a copy of all the contents. So let's examine the phone for any trade secrets – Brenda you'll need to take the lead on discovering things on Randy Chen's phone that your company wouldn't want to be shared with the world. If we find something that might lead to someone's arrest or prosecution, then we'll definitely share with them at some point, but remember they likely lack the resources to unlock it. The police may request phone records from the telecom provider in the United States. I'm not sure how that works – maybe they ask their embassy to help in the U.S. We need some time to look at the phone's data ourselves. "

"Are we required by law to share it with them immediately?" Marie asked. "I'd rather not spend any time in an Italian jail."

"I don't know. I wonder if Henrik has an attorney on his staff that could loosely answer the questions for us. Part of the problem for me is I think about the Amanda Knox murder conviction that took four years to overturn and I remember how bad the forensic evidence was handled by overzealous cops. I don't have a feel yet for our threesome. On the one hand, I think poorly of their investigative skills, but on the other hand if you don't have exotic murders like Randy Chen's, your brain just doesn't think in that manner."

"I'll give Henrik a call and see if we can get an answer before our meeting this afternoon," Marie said.

"Okay maybe the three of us can focus on Randy's phone. I thought we would start with his texts. Angela and Brenda, I need help checking out phone numbers and people. Let's try and plot who Randy spoke to starting with the day of his death and moving backwards. Let's devote a separate piece of butcher paper to tracking his movements," Jill said pointing at a wall.

"I wonder why the killer or killers left Randy's phone with him?" Marie asked. "Were they unsophisticated in not understanding how much information was likely on the phone or did they leave his wallet and phone to make sure it looked like an accident?"

"Good questions – add those to our chart on the questions section."

CHAPTER 8

Jill, Brenda, and Angela were staring at Jill's laptop screen reviewing the copy of Randy Chen's cell phone data. It was the first time Jill looked at data on a cell phone on her laptop and it was only the second case where she resorted to using cell phone information to gain insight into a case. It was weird to look at phone information in this manner. They were thankful that they had a charger for the cell phone and hadn't had to struggle with a dead battery.

"I'm confused as to whether we should start with email and go backwards in time from the last email or look at all his texts in the same manner?" Angela said. "Then there's attachments and links to follow with some of these communications."

Jill thought for a few moments and said, "Why don't we sort all of his emails, texts, and phone calls into the descending order they occurred starting with his last communication on the phone. So what is the last communication?"

"Are we sure we want to concentrate on just those three?" Marie said rejoining them after her phone call. "How about Facebook, Twitter, Viber, WhatsApp, and any other applications he seemed to be using? For all we know, he could have arranged a meeting on Viber."

"You're right and this is getting even more complicated. Let's take a quick look at these apps and see which ones he was using recently. Then perhaps we'll each take a few apps and plot out their timelines until we figure out his communication style. Were you able to get any lawyer advice from Henrik?"

"Yes and no. Henrik has had some interactions with Italy on the business side and his advice was to give them the phone immediately, but not mention we had unlocked and copied it. Italy isn't known for IT sophistication so he doubted they can tell you copied the phone."

"Okay, I'll have to think about how to roll that into the conversation. I'd rather they ask me for it and I'll hand it over, so I need to think about how to set them up to ask that question."

"Since we all want to stay out of jail, why don't you spend some quiet time thinking about how to do that, while the three of us work on Randy's phone log," Marie suggested.

Jill nodded and went to the kitchen to get some coffee while her mind sorted through scenarios on how to hand over Randy Chen's phone with nonchalance to the prosecutor. Nathan exited their bedroom and entered the kitchen after giving a wave at the women working in the living room.

Jill passed her cup of coffee to him as she gave him a kiss and made a second cup for herself. Nathan really needed coffee in the morning as he was generally a night owl and was slow to awake in the morning. Just as she was taking her second sip a plan formed in her brain that was mostly the truth,

Melissa Chen must not have had a conversation with the Italian police or not mentioned that she mailed the phone to Jill as they hadn't asked for it. She'd ask Melissa to stay silent on whether they had been able to unlock her father's phone. She would simply tell the officers that she had asked Melissa to send the phone and hand it over. It would be even better if she could drain the battery and she could honestly say she didn't know the code to unlock it – she had used an expert to figure it out for her.

They copied Randy Chen's cell phone records onto each of their own laptops and were labeling the timelines of each of his various interactions with his phone on their own piece of butcher paper. Marie had been right that Randy Chen used multiple communication applications. Nathan sat nursing his second cup of coffee before asking if anyone wanted an early lunch before they left to walk to the University. After enthusiastic replies, he set forth making soup and sandwiches for Jill and her friends. He had his own meetings to attend as he'd arranged tours of several wineries in the region.

"Guys it's time to walk to the University," Jill said. "Brenda, text me if you see something unusual."

Brenda watched them go thinking about all the work they had discovered and all the evidence that was left to be discovered. She hoped she would notice something relevant and unusual for Jill, but she admitted that she didn't think like them. She felt the pressure of that confidence that Jill seemed to have in her to find the trail that would lead them to the new product that Randy had been chasing.

The three of them set off for the walk to their meeting location. It was a beautiful fall day in Sicily. The weather was sunny with just enough of a light breeze to require a lightweight sweater. Rain was forecasted for later in the week, which might wash away forensic evidence, but there was nothing she could do to stop the rain.

As they approached the entrance to the University, Jill saw Vice Questore Cavallaro waiting for their arrival.

"Ciao, Vice Questore. I'd say 'good afternoon' in Italian but sadly I only know good morning and good night," Jill said. "This is Marie Simon, the other member of my team that you haven't met. She's a maven at finding traces of people on the internet. I have one other team member who is a financial wizard, but she is not with us in Italy."

Jill didn't add the word 'yet' to her sentence.

Marie shook hands with Sara Cavallaro and then the policewoman directed them inside the University of Catania campus. Soon they were entering a building made of stone and marble looking several centuries old. Jill loved the interior of the old building. They passed a library filled with bone artifacts and texts arriving at a now empty student lecture hall. Jill posited the forensic expert must also be on the faculty of the University.

Cavallaro performed introductions, "This is Associate Professor Dr. Antonella Coli. She's our expert that we consult with in any difficult case," then she introduced Jill's team to the prosecutor and the professor.

Pubblico Ministero Lombardo said, "Dr. Quint, we have brought Dr. Coli into this case, not because we doubt your findings, but rather because she will understand how to use your findings in the Italian justice system."

"Okay. What would you like to know?"

Dr. Coli and Dr. Quint proceeded into a technical discussion of Jill's autopsy findings, her training, as well as what she found at the scene in the Mount Etna crater. The others just listened to the two doctors speak of pathology, toxicology, and falling bodies. They reviewed the blood results from Jill's Swiss lab. Dr. Coli nodded, listening.

At the end of Jill's explanation Coli said to Lombardo, "Mr. Chen was lucky to have Dr. Quint do his autopsy. As she's an expert in the United States, I believe we can use her autopsy results. However, I would recommend that new blood work be extracted from Mr. Chen's remains and sent to the toxicology lab in Rome. I'm sure we can work out a chain of custody documentation to follow the sample from the United States back to Italy, no?"

Tenete Rosso said, "Yes we have spoken with the police in his hometown and we have agreed in principle to a chain of custody."

Lombardo asked, "Dr. Coli is there any other evidence we should collect that you haven't seen here?"

Coli asked Jill to review the data once again and ten minutes later she said to Lombardo, "No, she's got photographs of the scene and the autopsy findings and I can't think of anything else to add. It's very complete."

Jill sensed they were coming to an end of the meeting with the pathology professor and she was looking for an opening to give the Italian officials, Randy Chen's phone. First though she wanted to see if she could influence their next steps.

"So what are the next steps in this investigation for you?" She clearly addressed the 'you' to any of the three justice system representatives who might answer her question.

"We have reasonable proof that Mr. Chen was murdered, but we don't know where he was murdered, who did it, or why. So I would say our next steps are to find the answers to those questions," Lombardo said.

"How?" Jill thought she was stepping over the line asking the question, but she didn't care. They could choose to say, 'none of her business', or they might give her some honest answers.

"I don't wish to take up any more of Dr. Coli's time, perhaps we can step outside and discuss the answers to your question."

Jill nodded and then as she was about to leave, Dr. Coli asked, "Dr. Quint, would you have time to present your case to my students while you're in Sicily? It would be an excellent learning opportunity for my students in forensics."

"Probably, but I don't speak Italian. Would they understand my lecture in English?"

The professor nodded and they made arrangements for Jill to do the lecture.

Lombardo directed them outside to a quiet courtyard saying, "Let us talk a while longer. My office is in Palermo and so it would be inconvenient to hold a meeting there for you and your team Dr. Quint."

Jill nodded and they took their seats on benches. Angela and Marie hadn't said anything so far and were both quietly watching the proceedings.

"Dr. Quint, you asked us how we are proceeding and it would not be a practice in the Italian justice system to tell you, a relative stranger with no official role in the case from our point of view. However, your assistance thus far has helped us identify a murder that would have gone undetected. Sicily has a murderer in our community that we need to apprehend and sentence. So I would ask my esteemed colleagues to tell you of their next steps. I suspect you have your own next steps and it wouldn't do for you to be tripping over us."

"We will be contacting Mr. Chen's daughter to gain access to his cell phone records. We'll be looking for information on who he spoke with. We are under the assumption that this was not a random act of murder as his belongings contained his wallet with cash in it. Also, you asked a good question about how his body would have been transported to the crater during the brief snow-storm that preceded his discovery and so we will look into this," Cavallaro said. "What are you and your team working on at the moment?"

One good turn deserved another. Jill briefly debated on what to say about the phone. She opened her purse and pulled out the phone.

"Melissa Chen mailed this to me just before she left the country yesterday," passing the phone over.

"Dr. Quint, I will caution you that it is a criminal offense to interfere in an investigation in Italy by withholding evidence," Lombardo said, clearly angered at the cavalier mention of the cellphone.

"Ah, but you had not contacted me at the time that the cell phone came into my possession that there was actually a crime committed in Italy. In fact, I was notified this morning when the meeting was set up that you were opening an official inquiry. I believe you had no faith in my findings until Dr. Coli verified my conclusions. That meeting is at an end, and I have given you the phone. There is no interference on my part," Jill replied not willing to be intimidated by the prosecutor.

Russo and Cavallaro had both tried to open the phone, but failed while Jill and Lombardo were exchanging words.

"The phone is locked. Did the victim's daughter give you the passcode?"

"No, she doesn't know it."

Cavallaro sighed and said, "We will have to send it to our crime lab in Rome to see if they can unlock the phone."

"Are they successful at unlocking phones in your criminal cases?"

"I don't know. It's never come up before."

"Will you be able to get GPS records from the telecom company as to where the phone pinged Italian cellular towers?" Jill asked.

Cavallaro looked to the prosecutor for an answer as she hadn't tried to do that in her career before.

"Yes," was the abrupt response from the prosecutor and Jill could see he was still suspicious of them. Of course Jill was suspicious of them being able to solve the case on their own.

"What are your next steps Dr. Quint?" Rosso asked.

"We were going to use our police contacts in Mr. Chen's hometown to gain access to telecom records. We are also exploring a series of towns that Mr. Chen was rumored to be visiting while here in Sicily. There are seven of them and so this will keep us busy. Marie is also exploring Mr. Chen on social media to see if there are any clues there," Jill knew she was risking rebuke from the Italians, and so she added. "Also, I have a copy of the phone's contents and all of my team are exploring his activities to establish a timeline on the days leading up to his death."

She observed Lombardo getting red in the face again and he said, "I asked you not to interfere in this case. You are withholding evidence by not giving us the passcode!"

"Actually I don't know the passcode. I used a computer expert outside of Italy to unlock the phone. I copied its contents and the phone locked. I don't know the passcode. I can share our copy of the phone, but you only have my word that the contents are from his phone. It seems that you need your own expert to unlock the phone."

Cavallaro tried to play peacemaker by saying, "I would appreciate a copy of the information you state is from Mr. Chen's phone. While our experts unlock the phone, we'll begin exploring the contents as well."

Jill nodded and made arrangements with Cavallaro to send her the information.

Rosso asked about the towns.

"You mentioned some towns that Mr. Chen wanted to visit. What are those towns and do you know why he wanted to visit them?"

"His daughter mentioned that it was a town with Sicily in its name. When we looked up those towns, it turns out that there are likely six of them to visit. A seventh town is referred to by a different name so we crossed that one off his list as well as an eighth town where it snowed."

"Do you have any thoughts as to why he would visit any of these towns?"

"Yes," Marie said. "Mr. Chen has been a producer of natural supplements for going on thirty years and he thought he found a new substance here on the island. His family and colleagues did not know the name of whatever plant he was pursuing, nor did they know what the plant might be used for; only that the plant was abundant on Sicily but rarely found elsewhere."

"Okay, maybe we'll go back to the University to see what a

plant expert could tell us about a rare plant on this island. Who else wanted this plant?" Rosso asked.

"If we knew more about the plant, then we might have a motive, but we haven't figured that out yet."

"That information isn't on his phone?" asked Lombardo.

"It may be, but we hadn't discovered it before we came over here to see you," Marie said.

Soon the group broke up to go their separate ways, with Jill and her team discussing their conversation with the three Italians all the way back to their apartment.

CHAPTER 9

The three Italians watched the Americans leave the courtyard. Once they were sure they were out hearing range, he said, "They are as annoying as hell, but I do have to say that she has seen things that we missed and I have no doubt in my mind that this is a murder case," Cavallaro said.

"I'm also in the unhappy position of agreeing with you," Rosso said.

"You two sound like you're on her side," Lombardo said.

"Well sir, they have accelerated progress in this case which I appreciate, and we had better get to work if we want to get out in front of them. Let's discuss how the body got up to the crater. I think that's the easier thing to track rather than the cell phone contents," Cavallaro said.

"Yes. I believe it would have taken some kind of off-road vehicle. I don't think you get a dead body up the mountain even if you placed it in a motorcycle sidecar. When we rode up the mountain yesterday, that vehicle really rocked from side to side and some of those boulders required a high clearance. Let's check with the company to see if all of their cars can be accounted for at the time that Mr. Chen was transported to the crater. Let's also check with them to see if they have seen or know of other cars that can make that trek."

"What should we do with the phone?"

"By law, the phone company must unlock it for us, but we'll let Rome take care of that. We'll need it for the eventual court case to stack evidence. In the meantime, we should receive a copy soon of the phone's contents. Let's discuss what we should do with that information. We all have sophisticated phones that collect all kinds of information on our activities, internet searches, apps used, etc. I doubt that it will be as easy as seeing an appointment with his killer the day of Mr. Chen's murder. We also don't have a motive yet, and while we would normally look at the family first – I feel that since they called in this group of consultants to prove it was a murder, that mostly rules them out. Let's check the alibis and movements of family members. Hopefully that will be a short investigation as only the daughter was here in Sicily. I would like to understand his company better so we may understand if a motive comes from a business rival. Let's hope that our friends in any of the Cosa Nostra family are not behind this murder," Lombardo said.

"Yes. If that happens, we will have to provide protection for those women if they are still in Sicily. Their level of danger goes down dramatically if they leave Sicily, perhaps we can work on encouraging them to leave," Rosso said.

"We should also check their credentials. We only have her word that she is a doctor of some repute in the United States. Let's see if we can check some references. We don't want her or her team interfering with a case that will go to trial in the future. I want to make sure she hasn't done that in the past. I'll take on that assignment while you work on transportation and phone data. What else should we be looking at?" Lombardo asked rubbing his head. This was turning into one of the most complex cases he'd overseen in years as a career prosecutor.

"Dr. Quint mentioned that she was researching cities that Mr.

Chen might have visited on the morning of his death. We'll add those to our list down the road. The list of cities is vague and we would have to rely on the citizens to have noticed Mr. Chen's presence. I think we will do better if we look at credit card purchases to see if he visited. We could ask the daughter for that information, but he may have kept pass-codes on his phone to access bank accounts and so that will get us the information faster. Will that method of obtaining data interfere with your court proceedings, sir?" Cavallaro asked.

"I think this case is going to set a new precedent in our system. I will need to consult with another judge to assure myself that we are making the correct decisions."

"I think we need more resources for this case. Specifically, some younger officers to track the activity on the phone. I say younger officers as I expect them to use their phones better than us three senior officers of the justice systems," Rosso advised.

"I agree," Cavallaro said.

"Yes, I believe we must set up an inquiry and bring additional help from each of our departments to this case, if for no other reason than to check that we are researching this case in accordance with the law. Let's regroup later this afternoon and every afternoon for the foreseeable future. I will find meeting space in Catania as this seems to be the hub of the case. We'll let our offices in Palermo know that we will be in the area for a while. Let's see if we can get a jump-start on those Americans!"

The three of them nodded and departed the courtyard with heads full of a massive to-do list and the excitement of a difficult case to solve.

CHAPTER 10

"So what do you think of the Italians so far?" Angela asked. "They seem competent in the laws of their country which I know to be different from other international cases. I like that they immediately used a countrywoman to verify my work. With Mr. Chen about to be buried, I considered that to be the most immediate thing to do in the near future and they recognized that, so kudos for them."

"But?" Marie said.

"They wasted hours before they contacted us in the first place and of course I was underwhelmed that no one asked the questions at the crater when Mr. Chen was first located there. You would have thought there would have been at least some investigation. I was also surprised that they didn't contact Melissa Chen for the phone. I think they need to add resources, so we'll see if they do. That will tell me they understand the complexity of this case. Then again they may easily locate the vehicle that took Mr. Chen's body to the crater, and then the case might be solved shortly."

"So our next steps are tracking his last movements?" Angela

suggested. "Or I could work on strictly looking for information on whatever plant captured Randy's attention."

"Great idea Angela! We have no idea what the motive is in this case, but we all suspect it is something related to his business. Melissa was the only person with access from his family to kill her father and she wouldn't have called us into the case if she'd committed the murder."

"I wouldn't believe Melissa to be the murderer even without evidence of her innocence. She doesn't have it in her," Angela said.

"She could be mentally ill and cover that up or be a high functioning sociopath," Jill suggested.

"Both mental illness and sociopath behavior are seen when someone is in their early twenties and trust me when I say I didn't see it in college, nor have I seen any strange behaviors when we've run into each other over the years."

"Okay, moving on. Is there any work for Jo to do? The company is privately held so I don't know if she'll be able to find much on it," Jill said.

"Why not ask her to check that box off, but like Angela I haven't heard of any company problems. They have a good record in the local community. Money may be at the heart of his murder, but we don't know where that source of money is to narrow the search for Jo."

Jill stopped a minute on the sidewalk to dictate a short message to Jo and then they finished the walk to the apartment.

Brenda looked up when they entered the apartment and Jill asked, "Did you discover anything interesting?"

"Not yet, but I tell you that this is very personal going through his communications. He's a complete gentleman in all his communications. Makes me want to re-think all my communications knowing that someday, someone might be reading them and judging any harsh words I text, or email."

"Oh sis," Marie said reaching over to give her sister a hug."As if you ever put harsh words in print."

"I try not to, but this has been a lesson and a motivation to stay on course,"

"So no mention of a new product he was sourcing?" Jill asked, reminding herself to avoid ever leaving a trail of regretful words.

"I've reached a place in his communications where he is referencing 'it'," Brenda said holding her hands up in quote marks, "But not what the 'it' is. I'm on the trail but it's a lot to sort through."

"I promised we would send the phone's contents to the police. You haven't seen anything that concerns you?"

"No, nothing...professional business conversations, fatherly conversations with Melissa, no trade secrets so far and even if there were, Sicily is so far off the beaten path from our company in Green Bay that it would take years to become a competitor to any of our secrets. An important business thing you can't see on Randy's phone is access to the company's mainframe. Our IT department set our phones up so that we can log in and view items on the mainframe, but anything read on our phones is erased. I'd be concerned if the police had access to our mainframe as there are all kinds of information with company secrets there."

"That's good. Okay, I'll send the phone's contents to Cavallaro and Rosso. Did Randy speak a Chinese dialect?"

"Not that I ever heard," Brenda said. "His parents were born in the United States, so I don't know that he grew up in a house that spoke Chinese. He's traveled to China, but I don't recall him saying he could speak Mandarin or Cantonese. Certainly, I've seen no evidence of communication in the Chinese alphabet."

"Okay, that's good. That complication we didn't need on having to translate some messages," Jill said.

"There are a few with some Italian in them, but I think it might be company tag-lines or otherwise marketing stuff, but Angela can take a look at it."

"Show me," Angela said with relish, eager to use her Italian language skills.

They were all quiet as Angela checked a few messages and nodded.

"Yeah, Brenda is correct. The Italian is a part of the signature line and it gives us the title of the person and or the company which may be relevant later if they're communicating on our mystery product, but not in the communications that Brenda showed me."

Jill nodded, "Okay Brenda you keep searching for mention of the mystery product as Angela called it, and that has a nice ring to it. Marie, Angela, and I will continue working on the timeline. Tomorrow, I'd like to begin looking at the cities on our list, so also keep an eye for a mention of a city with the name of Sicily in its title. It could even be in the signature line of one those Italian signature emails."

Dusk was approaching when Nathan returned to the apartment from his winery tour bringing with him a case of wine. The women took a break from the tedious work they had been at, standing up and stretching, then going over to Nathan's case to see what he'd bought.

Angela went for wine glasses and a corkscrew ready to dive into Nathan's selections.

"Is this wine from the wineries you visited?" Marie asked.

"Yes and no. Some bottles are from wineries that I might be interested in doing business with. I also asked for wine recommendations for Jill's new grape, if the winery didn't offer it as a varietal. I even have one bottle specifically for Jill. It was too sweet for my palate, but it should be right up her alley."

She leaned in to kiss him saying, "I do like a man that understands my taste buds. Which bottle is it?"

"If you start with that bottle, it will dull your palate for sampling the Nero d'Avola grape as it's less sweet. Let's start with the bottles of your grape and then you can have your sweet wine after dinner. Deal?"

"Deal. What are you cooking for dinner?" Jill asked.

"Maybe you want to cook tonight?" Nathan suggested.

"No!" Marie and Angela exclaimed at the same time.

"I'd be insulted, my friends, but I happen to agree with you. Why would I ever attempt to cook when we have a maestro in the kitchen!"

"In that case, we'll have the cuttlefish that I picked up in the market earlier. I thought I would do a spicy crust with pistachio nuts, a salad, couscous, and apples and cheese for dessert. Why don't we sample the wines and you can tell me what you've been up to today."

"Actually, we could use a brain break. Why don't you describe the wineries you visited and what you liked about them," Angela suggested and the others nodded. "Also tell how on an island of so many wineries, that you picked the ones that you did."

"Ladies, those are good questions. Give me a moment to organize our wine tasting."

He pulled out four bottles that Jill assumed were made from her grape of interest. He turned the labels away from them and then reached in the cabinet for plastic cups. He poured five glasses for each bottle and lined them up in front of them.

"Let's let the wine breathe for about forty-five minutes and I'll tell you about my day."

"Can I come work for you, Jill? You get to visit exotic locations, eat great food, do expert wine tastings and make money," Brenda said.

"Moments like this when Nathan is cooking and we're wine tasting make up for the times when we nearly die when the bad guys are chasing us," Angela said with a smile.

"There is that downside," Marie agreed with a grin.

Jill all of a sudden got teary-eyed and had to hug each of her friends and Nathan.

"Sorry about that, but you guys mean the world to me. Love you."

"We love you back," Angela and Marie rejoined.

"Okay ladies, move beyond the mush or I won't know what to do. So in answer to Angela's earlier question, I chose the wineries based on a variety of attributes. They needed to be producing for five years at a minimum, I read their reviews, they have someone who speaks English, I checked their wine labels, and I wanted to see that they were growing as a vineyard. From there, I knocked my list down further by trying to organize them by a geographic area. This island is big and I knew I didn't have time to reach the wineries near Palermo in a half day."

"Were you disappointed with any of the wineries?" Angela asked.

"Yes, one had a dirty tasting room. The wine was excellent, but I worried about the bottle quality when no one was paying attention to the cleanliness of what the public sees. I spared a thought as to whether the wine might be dirty as well, but then I figured the alcohol content would kill off most of the dangerous bugs."

"Did you buy a bottle from them or say anything about the cleanliness?" Marie asked. It was so refreshing to talk about Nathan's day rather than the deep dive they had been doing into Randy Chen's life.

"I debated whether to say something. The last thing most Sicilians want is American arrogance in telling them how to run their business. I was all by myself there and so I took a chance. I really liked their wine, but I could see that they were struggling. So I offered to help them with marketing and in return they had to fix their tasting room. At first they were suspicious, but then I drew them a wine label and showed them my website. They in turn showed me a sticker they have on the tasting room door. It signifies that they don't pay protection money to the local mafia. It was really quite sad. This island needs financial help, but the mafia really has their hands in everyone's pockets."

"Wow, I'd love to see you boost the small guy and make them a success and thumb your nose at the mafia. Do you think you can do it?" Jill asked.

"I do. I need to take Angela there soon so we can get some photos, but I bet I can get them on the right track quickly. In return, I'll get some good wine and I'll even create a route for them to export to the United States which will further gain them sales away from the mafia."

"We planned to visit the cities tomorrow with Sicily in their name and I wanted to take Angela in case I needed Italian translation. The cities are mostly around the base of Mount Etna, but I don't have a sense of distance to know if I could visit them all in a day. Besides I need a little more pinpointing than just randomly showing up and asking residents if they ever met Randy Chen."

"I might be able to help you narrow that down Jill, I've found two of the cities on your list in Randy's emails, but I'm not through looking," Brenda said.

"Yeah, I might have found one as well. Hopefully it's the same one that Brenda saw," Marie said.

"So tomorrow we'll mix business and pleasure. We travel out to your winery. I just checked the weather and the perfect time for me to shoot outdoors is about noon. So I'd like to understand what you and the client want and I need some time to set-up, so we need to be there no later than 11:15. I like the thought of helping a small business stand up to the big guns of the mafia, and so if you were wondering if I would charge for my services the answer is 'no'."

"Okay, let's plan on leaving here at nine tomorrow to visit my cities first. Depending on how the day's going we'll either drop the two of you off to conduct your business, so we'll grab a picnic lunch along the way and take a break while you guys work," Jill suggested.

"Sounds like a plan! The wine should have breathed enough to begin our tasting," Nathan said picking up his plastic cup and inviting the ladies to do likewise. "Cheers!"

Forty minutes later, they were all pleasantly mellowed from the wine and they had ranked the wines.

"Nathan thanks for arranging these wine tastings. The fact that my favorite each time we taste a group of the Nero d'Avola varietal is the favorite of the four of you suggests to me that I can create this varietal at home. You've boosted my confidence with the grape. As you know I was concerned that this is a less sweet wine as compared to what I've been producing, and I wasn't sure I had the palate to make the varietal. Now, I think I can, and so when I get home I'm going to plant this new grape."

They all toasted to that news.

CHAPTER 11

Jill and Marie were up early the next morning as was their habit. The previous night they'd come across additional information on the potential cities that Randy Chen had visited. They were able to confidently reduce their list of seven down to three cities. They printed multiple copies of Randy Chen's picture so if they had the opportunity, they could ask townspeople if they'd seen him. Jill had also asked Melissa to check her father's credit and debit cards to see where he spent money on the island. She said she would, but she knew her father to try and pay for things with cash as the nation was poor. Meanwhile, Brenda was on to something that she thought might be the product.

It started with a reference in an email conversation to a tree that Randy was looking for. He asked several plant experts at the University and in the Department of Agriculture for the location of a specific plant. Jill didn't immediately recognize the Latin name of the plant and so had to look it up. It was a derivative of oldenlandia adscensions. Why would Randy choose oldenlandia adscensions? It was widely distributed across the world for a variety of purposes and Jill could see no revolutionary discovery in regards to that plant. Brenda had also seen references to olives and bee products. She touched base with her marketing department back home to see what they were aware of and all they had done was some theoretical product projections on market size. They had no name for the product or even how it was to be used – with the mention of oldenlandia adscensions. Jill thought there would be a reference to a lotion in some conversation as that was typically how the plant was used. Brenda had to call it quits for the night as she been looking at Randy's communication for hours and was bug-eyed with fatigue. Jill was interested in seeing what more Brenda would find today working in the apartment while they were exploring the countryside.

Angela arrived from her bedroom looking rested and refreshed and joined them in working after she rechecked her photographer's bag that she had everything she needed for a photo shoot that day.

The timeline was complete for all of the communications they had that occurred during the last twenty-four hours of his life. He had an appointment for the morning of his death at an unknown address, but there was no indication whom he was meeting with. Randy Chen was superstitious about new products according to Brenda. Besides the meditating he liked to do next to a product, he avoided mentioning the product or his contacts until he made a decision on a product. So his calendar on his phone had shown blocks of time for apparent meetings with no further information. Little did the man know that his system would be such a total failure for investigators trying to figure out who murdered him.

Nathan stumbled out of his and Jill's bedroom to the kitchen like a homing pigeon on a mission for a cup of coffee. Jill looked up and smiled at Marie as they were all aware that Nathan's one downside was he wasn't a morning person and therefore he could have no conversation until he consumed his first cup of coffee.

Brenda would contact the people that Randy spoke with on behalf of the company to see if she could ferret out the content of his conversation. If she didn't get anywhere then Jill might try making the connection later herself. Marie, who was a master gardener at home, was also in line to talk with the plant experts if necessary, but like Jill she was puzzled over Randy Chen's excitement for the plant.

Jill saw an incoming email from Melissa Chen and checked her watch. Poor woman, she must not be getting any sleep as it was the middle of the night in Wisconsin. The message was filled with the information she was looking for – Randy Chen had multiple purchases over the past seven months at a town named Fiumefreddo di Sicilia. Jill was hopeful that this was a town where Randy might have met with his killer.

"Hey, there's a chance we have found out the city where Randy's product was located. It's called Fiumefreddo di Sicilia. I'm glad I don't have to type that name in on all my internet purchases for the delivery address. Marie maybe you can search the town as we travel there. I would do so, but I'll get carsick."

"Okay, but what are we going to do once we reach the town? I don't recall us ever having so vague a reason to visit a town and search for information," Marie replied.

"You're right, we haven't had so vague a reason before. I asked Melissa for the names of the establishments where Randy made purchases. We'll approach each establishment with Randy's picture and ask if the person remembers an American who looks like the picture. If they do, let's ask if he was with someone or by himself and then let's ask if they know of anyone in town that spoke with him."

"And if they ask us why we're asking those questions?" Marie asked.

"Then I think we have two choices," Angela said. "We could tell them he was murdered and we've been hired to find his murderer. Or we could say he passed away and we are from his company and trying to follow his trail to a new product he was excited about."

They had taken seats in their car and Nathan was at the wheel and said, "Ladies, don't forget this is Sicily. The government is often corrupt and the mafia rules. I think Angela's second suggestion will get you more cooperation from the Fiumefreddo residents than the stark truth of the first explanation. I had a sense of the fear of both from my winery owners. They are so frustrated that the island doesn't run better because of corruption."

"That's a good point, sweetie," Jill said impressed with his logic. "I forget how deep the distrust is here on this island. I hope the mafia isn't involved in our case, but in the brief reading I did last night it seems like they have eyes, ears, and hands spread everywhere on this island. If they didn't know about us before, they soon will after we spend time asking questions."

"They may even resent us more once Angela and I help this winery out with their marketing, so the two of us may become separate targets from your team," Nathan cautioned.

"Okay, now you're scaring us, Nathan," Angela said from the back seat.

"All I'm saying is this is a wonderfully bucolic island, but don't be fooled and drop your guard. This is a more dangerous place than Edinburgh or Brussels, or Breckenridge was and some of us nearly died in those cities!"

"Okay, those are words of wisdom. Maybe it's time to think of weapons. Let's stop by a drugstore or grocery store and see if we can find any cans of something toxic to spray in someone's eyes. If we can't then let's find a toy store and get some water pistols and I'll make a pepper juice spray that we can carry in self-defense," Jill suggested.

There was silence in the car for a while as they all digested the potential danger that could befall them in the land owned by the mafia.

"Here's another piece of unhappy news, this town that we're going to had some scenes from the movie, 'The Godfather' filmed there," Marie said studying her phone.

"I've never watched that film as I always considered it too violent, but I do remember seeing clips from the dinner scene where the music so matched the violence," Jill said.

"Okay, I'll move the conversation to happier subjects. The town means cold river in Italian and it's named for a cold river that comes from the snow melt of Mount Etna," Angela said looking at her phone, "Which I should have figured out."

"I wondered where such a weird name came from so Freddo means river and Fiume means cold?" Jill asked.

"Actually you have the words reversed – Freddo means cold."

"Yes, that reaffirms that I have little talent for languages," Jill said with a laugh.

"There are about 10,000 residents that live in this town, so we won't be able to question them all," Marie said.

"No, we won't and let's not forget we're limited by language. These smaller towns are more likely to have residents that speak Italian only. Let's fan out around the locations Randy made purchases at. We can only hope that this town was his final destination. We'll have about ninety minutes there before we need to move on to the winery? Is that correct Nathan?" Jill asked.

"Yes, that's about right. The two locations are about twenty minutes apart. Perhaps the winery owner knows something of Randy Chen. Do you know if he drank wine?"

"He was a health nut, but Marie or Angela, do you remember seeing him drink around town?" Jill asked.

"Let me text Brenda and see if she knows," Marie said.

"Great idea!"

A short time later, Marie announced, "Randy drank wine and has a large wine cellar in his home."

"I may have to ask Melissa to look and see if Randy has any bottles from Sicily. That might give us more information. But rather than have her look through a potentially large collection, we'll see if we can find information in other ways."

"Perhaps some of his receipts were for wine purchases or

maybe he kept a digital catalog of his wine. I know many connoisseurs do that as there's no other way to keep track of say two or three-thousand wine bottles," Nathan suggested.

"I'll ask Brenda about that as she was over to his house many times," Marie said.

"Have you given thought to who might be behind Randy's murder?" asked Angela.

"I have. The first set of suspects should be his family, but everyone has an alibi there."

"Besides they don't seem like a family that would kill their father," Angela added.

"As good detectives we can assume anything, but their alibis were checked and so I don't need to do any more work with them. I also don't believe this was a random act of violence as his valuables weren't removed and the method of killing him took some preplanning. So the top of my list is this substance he was chasing - someone else must have had their eye on it too. Since this is Sicily, my number one suspect is organized crime."

"Oh," muttered Jill's other three passengers.

"Perhaps we shouldn't pursue this case from the island of Sicily. Could we do it long distance from the United States?" Marie asked.

"No, we need boots on the ground here. We can't visit these towns or run into people and interview them over the phone. We'll be safe."

Angela and Marie looked at each other and Marie said, "We don't believe you!"

"Ditto," added Nathan from the driver's seat. "In fact I'm suspicious of a car that's been following us since we left the apartment. What are the odds of that?"

All three woman whipped their heads around to look at who was following them.

CHAPTER 12

A sedan car was indeed behind them. Jill studied the driver and said, "I think that's a woman at the wheel. I don't believe the mafia uses women in Sicily."

"You would be wrong, Jill. I just visited a site that said that there are over 150 women in Italian jails for Mafioso activities," Marie said with an edge to her voice.

"Uh oh," Jill said and then added to Nathan, "If I knew where we were, I'd steer you towards help in case she's from the Mafioso."

"We're coming into our first town. I'll pull into the first place I see to park," Nathan said.

The sedan passed them by, even though there was space to pull in behind Nathan's car.

"Originally, I thought we should split up and question people, but in light of the sedan, let's pair up. As Nathan and Angela are the better Italian speakers, why don't you go with Nathan?" Jill said looking at Marie in the back seat.

"Sure! It's nice to be guarded by a Master Black Belt, but how about you ladies?"

Jill opened her purse and pulled out an aerosol can with Italian words on it.

"It seemed wise to have some weapon here in Sicily, so I had Nathan get a couple of cans of bug spray so we would have some weapon here, yet not violate the law. Here's a can for you Marie, I've got a second inside my purse."

"No can for me?" Angela asked.

"You never carry a purse big enough to conceal such an item," Jill said pointedly looking at Angela's purse.

"Maybe I'll start to carry around my photographer's bag as it's big enough to contain that can."

"Okay, we have a third one at the apartment. I didn't bring it with me as I didn't think we would run into trouble so soon. I didn't get a clear look at the woman in the sedan. We could pass her in the street and I wouldn't recognize her. Do either of you have a better description?"

"I'll recognize her by the sunglasses. I saw them in a Ferragamo store in the Rome airport on the way here and tried them on," Marie said.

"Did you buy them?" asked Angela.

"No, they were too expensive, but they sure looked good on my face."

"How about her shirt or hair color, could you see that?"

"Not for sure. She had dark hair, but whether black or brown I couldn't tell. As for clothing, it was also dark," Angela said.

"I watched her frequently in the rearview mirror and she has a nervous tick of moving her hair behind her right ear frequently if that helps," Nathan said.

"We don't have much of a description. Marie can you send me a picture from the Ferragamo store of the sunglasses you saw so Angela and I can recognize them?"

They set off in pairs towards an area ahead that had lots of pedestrian traffic hoping it was the main street. They split off to opposite sides of the street planning to walk the length of the first block and see what businesses it contained.

Three blocks later they had visited a pharmacy, a real estate office, a cake shop, a florist and a pizzeria. Their time was up and all they had to show for their efforts was a cupcake from the cake store. No one recognized the picture of Randy Chen.

It was time to return to the car and head for the winery. Jill debated splitting up as they hadn't finished with the town, but she was thinking they were wasting their time without having the information of the receipts for Randy's purchases in Sicily. The town though small by her standards, still contained too many businesses for this to be a valuable use of their time. In fact, they weren't sure he'd made any purchases in the town, just that Brenda saw mention of the city in an email. Melissa Chen hadn't known her father's banking password and had to jump through some legal hurdles before getting Jill the information hopefully later that day.

After walking back to the car, Angela asked, "Not to be pessimistic, but don't the mafia plant car bombs in Sicily?"

They all halted in their tracks wondering what to do next. Each did a quick Google search to understand common tactics for killing people in Sicily by the mob.

"I don't see any use of car bombs since the 1990s," Marie said. They relaxed a little with that news.

"Let's back up and I'll start by hitting the door unlock on the key fob," Nathan said.

"If the car survives that, then how about if we all look under the carriage and the hood, to see if anything was planted there," Jill added. "We'll look like idiots to the traffic going by, but I'd rather appear dumb than dead."

They backed so far away that the key fob didn't register so Nathan moved closer to hit the button. He did and nothing happened. He repeated several more times with car honking to acknowledge it was locked, followed by the doors unlocking.

Then they were all flat on the pavement looking under the car and they didn't see anything. Finally Nathan opened the door and unlocked the hood where they found nothing unusual.

"If anyone was watching us from any windows around here I'm sure we've been labeled with the title 'Crazy Americans'," Marie said with a grin.

"Like Jill said, better to be dumb than dead," Angela added smiling.

Twenty minutes later they turned into a driveway to a winery. Jill's first thought was 'this is better than California'. A couple came out of a building as Nathan parked the car. He performed introductions and Jill found herself kissing the cheeks of Giacomo and Carmela Milo, the owners of the winery.

The winery was beautiful. There was a field of grapevines with leaves turning into fall colors leading up to the base of Mount Etna. A Mediterranean building housed their wine barrel room and grape processing area. They had a small tasting room with bottles on the shelf for tasting. Angela stood looking at the scenery in front of her, thinking about what Nathan said he wanted to capture in the wine label and marketing materials. She could work with this landscape. She took her photographer's bag from the trunk. After a conversation in English with Giacomo and Carmella searching for English words and Angela helping, they determined that Jill and Marie would settle at an outdoor picnic table where they would have internet access from the winery as well as wine and cheese at their leisure. Nathan and Angela would meet with the owners and then Angela would roam finding the photography angles she needed. The Milos had planned to serve them lunch after Nathan and Angela finished their work. Angela informed the Milos she also wanted pictures of them in their vineyard, barrel room and next to the vines. Later that afternoon Carmelo made a Sicilian lunch consisting of fish, pasta, salad, and more wine. They were all ready for a nap after the relaxing hours at the vineyard.

They were getting ready to open their car doors when Jill asked offhandedly, "Giacomo, Carmella, you didn't by chance meet this man?" while holding out a picture.

They looked at the picture and then at each other before Carmela said, "Yes, he stopped by our winery one day and purchased a few bottles. I remember because it was a slow day and he seemed so kind and interested in our wines. It's rare that we get Americans here by themselves. They usually travel in groups."

"Did he say why he was in the area or where else he visited in Sicily?" Jill asked urgently. Then Angela took over and had a detailed conversation with the couple while she took notes. Jill was dying to know what was said, but she knew Angela would get more detail out of them in their native language rather than Jill questioning them in English. A person's language was always richer when it was their first language.

Angela ended the conversation and they piled into the car to head off. Melissa sent an email with businesses related to charges on her father's credit card while Jill and Marie had worked at the picnic table, and now they had a new itinerary of cities to visit based on those receipts. While Nathan set his GPS to head to the first location, Jill leaned over the front seat anxious to hear what Angela had discussed with the Milos.

"He spent about two hours tasting their wines and purchased a case to be shipped back home. He doesn't speak Italian, so their conversation was slow and comical as each of them searched for the right words or gestures to indicate what they meant. They asked him if he was on vacation in Sicily, and he said no it was a business trip, but he'd built in leisure time. He said he manufac- tured natural vitamins, lotions and potions and he was looking for raw materials.

"They asked him if he was looking for olive oil and Randy said yes. A little later in their conversation they spoke of honey and again Randy was interested."

"I wonder if he was interested in olive oil or bee products to meditate with or just with curiosity as to what other businesses were doing on this island?" Marie questioned.

Jill nodded, "Good question. Was he passionate about their substances or just professionally curious."

"Yes I wondered at the Milos replies as olive oil and honey are found everywhere and I had oldenlandia adscensions in the back of my mind. I asked a few more questions but couldn't get any more clarity on the topic, but their guess was professional curiosity. Of course, they said it was an intense conversation as they had to work so hard to understand each other and they can't always translate the behavior of non-Sicilians."

"So their conversation is helpful to our case, but not helpful," Jill surmised.

"Except they added one more thing, he asked about that notice on the tasting room's door – the one that says they don't pay protection money to the mafia. Giacomo said maybe a third of their conversation was devoted to that subject which they thought unusual. Most people are like Nathan, they ask about the notice, and then the conversation moved on beyond the mafia once they explain their situation on the island. That was also why Randy was so memorable as it was an unusual conversation."

"Hmmm," Jill said.

"That's not good news," added Marie. "I don't want to face that group. They'll follow us back to Wisconsin. We'll never get rid of them if we hit their radar screen."

"Ladies, we're coming upon the first business on your list. I've not noticed anyone following us this time. I'm going to find parking."

All three women turned their attention to the rear window of the car as though to verify the absence of a car following them, as Nathan came to a stop.

CHAPTER 13

"We haven't seen the woman in the sedan since that last small town. Either it was random bad luck that she was following us from Catania and heading to roughly the same destination or she's placed a tracker on our car and knows where we've been," Jill said. "Nathan or Angela can you call the Milos later to see if anyone stops by this afternoon to question them about us? A little paranoia on my part will help keep us safe."

Marie, Angela, and Nathan all gave her a silent facial gesture suggesting she was perhaps too late to look out for their safety.

"Okay guys, you're right that we seem to be dragged into dangerous situations before I ever give you a chance to say you don't want to be there. This time it's Marie's fault as she brought the case to us!"

"True," Marie agreed. "We could call Melissa up and say we think the mafia might be involved and we're going to leave the case to the authorities."

"No!" came three replies from her colleagues.

"I need to go back to the winery in two days to go over my plans with them," Nathan said.

"I know Randy on behalf of our community and I think we need to solve his murder," Angela said.

They were standing on the sidewalk next to car during this last conversation, Jill spread her arms for a group hug, "I want to solve this case as we're eons ahead of the Italian police. We're needed here. Marie, you could fly to Rome and be close-by, but safe and still help us."

"I'm good, I was just doing a gut-check with you guys and I got my answers," she said with a smile as they all leaned out of the hug. "Let's go question this store where Randy made a purchase."

Walking down the street, they found a pharmacy that sold products for colds and other ailments that also contained a fairly large section devoted to honey and bee pollen products. Angela was the lead in all of their interviews as she was the best at gleaming information from people and she had the added advantage of speaking Italian.

Nathan stayed outside watching for their mysterious sedan. Marie was hunting for a new lip balm among the bee products and Jill was looking for an anti-nausea product that wouldn't make her sleepy as she'd forgotten to pack her carsickness medication before leaving for Italy. Jill and Marie approached the cashier as Angela was winding down her conversation with her. They paid for their products and left, choosing not to say anything until they were once again in the car.

"She remembered him as he'd asked so many questions about the bee pollen products that the pharmacist had to come from behind the counter to answer. He wasn't there today, but will be tomorrow morning, so I think we'll have to come back. The clerk either couldn't hear their conversation or was too polite to share information with strangers – I couldn't tell."

"So maybe he was after a bee pollen product?" Jill suggested. "Marie, can you check with Brenda to see if she remembers any product conversations around bee pollen?"

"Sure."

"Are bees different in Sicily?" Nathan asked.

Angela had been doing bee research during the discussion and said, "The most common honey bee for global beekeepers are Italian bees. A website lists their pluses and minuses and that they're popular in the United States. However, if we already have Italian bees, why would Randy Chen need to go to Sicily for bee pollen?"

"And are Sicilian bees different from mainland Italy bees?" Jill asked.

"I don't see the answer to your question here, but I'm guessing there's no difference."

"Brenda said the company has bee pollen products already and perhaps Randy was just exploring growing techniques or a variety of products made from pollen."

"That's sort of my feeling about bee pollen – the market seems saturated so why would Randy Chen be so excited over such an ordinary product," Jill said.

"Remember though we thought he might be looking at olden-landia adscensions and that's another overdone product," Angela said.

"Okay let's move on to the next location. If I recall from our internet search, it's an olive oil retailer," Jill said giving Nathan the address for his GPS.

"Currently Randy's company sells olive oil in their retail stores, but it is someone else's brand. His company does not manufacture olive oil for retail sales," Marie said.

"So maybe he's thinking of expanding into olive oil, but since he already has it in his retail stores, you wonder about his excitement and passion for a new product," Angela said. "It doesn't feel like a product worth meditating on. Olive oil is used for cooking as it's a better fat than many other things, but I've never heard of taking an olive oil capsule for a body ailment. Have you?"

"No, but I'll do a search later just to verify. I recall reading about studies on lowering cholesterol with extra virgin olive oil, but again there's lots of olive oil in the world and Italian trees aren't special, and Mr. Chen can't grow olive trees in Wisconsin to make his own olive oil from scratch. I could see him purchasing generic olive oil and bottling it as his own, but that's not a revolutionary product," Jill said. "I guess all we can do at this location is to ask about his conversation with the store owner."

"Okay while Angela asks questions, I'm shopping for olive oil," Marie said.

"I'll stay outside with Nathan and watch our surroundings."

Twenty minutes later they were all back in the car, Jill and Nathan having observed the sedan pass by once.

It was time to head back to their apartment as the next receipt to chase after was in a town on the other side of Mount Etna and by the time they got there, the business might no longer be open.

"I just remembered I included a scanner in my autopsy case now, and so when we get home I want to scan this car. I'm worried that we saw the woman driving the sedan car. This was our third stop in a different town, how would she know where we are? I don't believe in coincidence in this case," Jill said.

"I agree with you," Nathan said glancing at the rear view mirror. "We'll start checking the car every time we start it."

There was silence in the car as everyone digested the worry about the woman driver. None of them believed it was an accident.

Jill broke the silence with, "Did you learn anything from the olive oil proprietor?"

"The owner remembers Randy, but said he seemed interested in learning about the olive oil they sold and nothing more despite my approaching the question from multiple directions. So this visit was a dead end," Angela said.

"Well I did get some tasty olive oil we can enjoy later," added Marie.

CHAPTER 14

Lombardo, Rosso, and Cavallaro were seated in a small conference room table in the Questora in Catania looking over the results they had obtained from an Italian lab from Mr. Chen's blood removed from his body in the United States. For a future court case, they had an excellent chain of custody documentation for this blood specimen unlike the good doctor.

"With our lab showing the presence of chloroform and the other physical findings, we have the evidence we need to prove this was a homicide," Lombardo said. "Now we need a suspect. What do you have?"

"We started with trying to track down how the body was moved to the crater. As we know at the time there was a brief snowstorm. I checked with our weather service and this was predicted in the forecast that day so we think it was likely part of the plan as at any other time, hikers would have seen the body dumped in the crater," Cavallaro said.

"We checked with all of the licensed carriers for the mountain and none report driving in that snowstorm let alone taking a passenger and a dead body," Rosso said.

"We then checked with an expert to find out if a pick-up truck with special tires could have made the journey. The answer is yes. Also a snowmobile or an all-terrain vehicle could make the journey. We checked with our weather service and the snowstorm on Mount Etna had been predicted for several days and our park authorities had informed the outfitters that they would be unlikely to lead tour groups that entire morning. It turned out to be a narrower window than the park staff predicted, still it would have been deadly for hikers alone as the visibility was poor and the ground slippery. Vehicle sounds were heard at times by our park staff, but they couldn't narrow the sound to a type of vehicle nor did they see anything," Lombardo said.

"Did they see any unexpected vehicles in the parking areas?" Lombardo asked.

"As tour groups arrive all day from around the island, the park staff pay little attention to the vehicles parked there," Rosso said. "The storm decreased visibility to the degree that it was hard to see more than about fifty meters in front of you."

"So you're saying that running down the vehicle that carried Mr. Chen to the crater is a wasted effort?" Lombardo said.

"Not at all sir. We just need more time. We have a report coming that lists of all the snow-mobiles and all-terrain vehicles registered in Sicily. I'm hoping the list is small as there's not a lot of use for such vehicles here.," Cavallaro said.

"How about Chloroform? Is it hard to obtain in Sicily or even in Italy?" Lombardo asked.

"It's a lab substance so in theory you need a lab license to buy it. It's also used as a refrigerant for older refrigerators," Rosso said. "Before you ask, we have no refrigerator manufacturers on Sicily, however, it's used by appliance repair people to recharge older refrigerators and car air conditioning. There are fifteen or so refrigerator makers on the mainland. The refrigerant comes in a canister as a liquid because it's compressed and I haven't heard back from my contact on how difficult it is to get the chloroform out of refrigerant. It can also be a product formed when you mix household bleach with acetone. I think this is a hard lead to run down if anyone with a little science can make it in their home."

"This is a complex case. Mr. Chen's murder was premeditated. It may have taken special effort to get chloroform and the vehicle to drop him in the crater in conjunction with a snowstorm. Brilliant. If the family hadn't hired Dr. Quint, we would have never known this was a murder," Lombardo said chagrin and disappointment in his voice.

"Agreed sir," Cavallaro said. "At least we had the sense to join the good doctor at the autopsy and built some rapport with her or we would be farther behind. I must say she's been helpful and cooperative, not trying to prove that we are idiots, though perhaps we are.... for failing to notice the suspicious circumstances of this crime."

There was quiet in the room as they thought about this statement.

"I have a press conference this afternoon to discuss this murder. I'll spend the rest of the afternoon preparing for the conference. We haven't discussed Mr. Chen's phone. What have you learned from that?" asked Lombardo.

"It's curious that the cell phone was left with him on the crater. While this murder was clearly planned in advance, this appears to be a stupid moment," Rosso said.

"Perhaps," replied Cavallaro. "It wouldn't have looked like an accident if his wallet and cell phone were missing from his person. Perhaps our murderer thought we would be unable to unlock the phone."

"True. Our lab experts are reviewing the phone and as you know we've provided the American phone company with a search warrant to track the pinging of the phone. We expect data within the next twenty-four hours. We're checking phone calls and texts to Italian numbers as we have immediate access to that data. There aren't very many phone calls as Mr. Chen did not speak Italian and so much can be arranged through the Internet even here in Sicily. We have one number that's suspicious as it appears to be an unregistered phone. Our crime scene techs in Rome are running that number down," Rosso said.

"Do you know what Dr. Quint is doing today?" Lombardo asked.

"We've had a tail on her. One of her team members, Angela Weber, has been speaking with merchants. We have word that she speaks Italian, so we will want to be careful around her if we think she can't understand what we're saying amongst ourselves. They also spent some time at a winery that does not seem to be connected to this case. We think they might be following a record of financial transactions they obtained from the family. I think I will call on them once they return to Catania and see if that is the case. If the doctor won't share the information with me, I'll reach out to the family. I plan to interview the doctor and her team to see what they've learned and evaluate whether we could do better getting information out of these merchants," Rosso said.

"Is she withholding information from you?" Lombardo asked.

"No, I don't think so, it's more like she received the information this morning and ran with it, before telling us. That's one of the reasons I want to visit her and her team in person to emphasize the fact that it's a crime to withhold evidence in Italy."

"I'm going to reach out to the Chen family as soon as this meeting is over to try and establish the same connection with the daughter that Dr. Quint seems to have. As the Americans say, we're late to this party and we need to make up for lost time," Cavallaro said.

"At this point, we don't have a motive for this murder and no suspects. Is that correct? I'll just discuss the circumstances of the murder during the press conference as we have little more to tell the public. Do either of you think the public is at risk?"

Both shook their heads and said "no."

"In my experience, sophisticated planned crimes are targeted at a single individual," Cavallaro said while Rosso nodded in agreement.

CHAPTER 15

Jill and the gang settled into their apartment living room. Jill had fetched the electronics detector she had packed into her autopsy case and they'd watched while Nathan scanned the car and found two bugs that appeared similar but different. The bugs were now sitting on the coffee table while the group searched for identifying information. Nathan identified them first while Angela leaned over his shoulder to read the Italian words.

"This says they are simple GPS trackers."

"Can you go to the website to see if there's a way to locate who is tracking the signal?" Marie asked.

Everyone looked over at her and Nathan quipped, "You sound like you've been reading spy novels!"

"Sorry gang, once you get into technical language on GPS, my Italian vocabulary doesn't go that far."

They were startled out of their thoughts when they heard a knock on the apartment door.

"Are you expecting anyone?" asked Nathan of the group.

After getting negative shakes of everyone's head, he approached the closed door and asked, "Who is it?"

Rosso standing on the other side of the door was startled to hear a male voice, but relaxed when he thought about the American accent he heard.

"This is Tenete Rosso and I would like to speak to Doctor Jill Quint."

Jill rose from her chair the moment she heard their guest say his name and nodded to Nathan to unlock the door.

When it opened to find the detective there, Jill asked, "Hello, detective, what can I do for you?"

"I would like to come in and speak with you and your team."

Jill nodded and opened the door wider. Rosso entered finding more people than he expected to find. He was about to ask for introductions, when his attention was caught by the numerous pieces of butcher paper taped to the wall.

"One moment," he said and he walked around the room reading the information on each paper. He pulled his cell phone out and began taking pictures.

"Lieutenant Rosso, do you not have something similar at your headquarters?" Jill asked.

"Yes in a different form, but I wanted to make sure we have all of the information that you do on these papers. In fact, that is what I'm here to talk to you about, but perhaps we could have introductions first. I'm Tenete Rosso of the Polizia and who are all of you? Your team is bigger than I expected."

"Yes, I have experts just as you do to help solve the mystery of Randy Chen's death," Jill said as she performed introductions. "Our final team member, Jo will arrive later tonight. She's the next best thing to a forensic accountant."

"I'm impressed with the variation in your team," he said and then looking at Angela, he said several sentences in Italian to which she nodded. She then said, "He asked if I spoke Italian considering that I interviewed merchants in Italian earlier today."

Jill reached over to grasp something on the coffee table and then held it out to Rosso and asked, "Did you or someone from the police place these GPS trackers on our car? We saw a woman in a red sedan in several towns and it couldn't have been a coincidence that she followed us, so we scanned the car for trackers when we returned to the apartment."

Rosso sighed and reached for the trackers in Jill's hand. After looking at both of them he said, "This one is ours, I wonder who placed the other tracker on your car?"

Jill didn't know whether to feel alarmed that two different groups were tracking their direction or mad that the police had been one of two trackers. Instead she repeated her question, "Was the woman in the sedan one of your officers?"

"No we don't use unmarked cars. We simply stopped at one of the shops you did to question the clerk on your conversation with them. That's how we learned that one of your team members speaks Italian. I stopped by here today to warn you that withholding information from the police is a criminal offense in Italy, perhaps that's different from the United States."

For some reason, Tenete Rosso's comment exploded the anger inside Jill. While she respected Rosso and Cavallaro, she was angry at the Italian law enforcement system's incompetence at detecting murders and she was especially affronted that her fellow pathologists were so poorly trained in Italy. So she spoke without censoring herself.

"Lieutenant Rosso, I notified your country of my intent to perform an autopsy before I arrived here inviting you to observe. I reasoned through a discussion with your pathology expert and with you on Mount Etna about the nature of Mr. Chen's injuries. It was the positive chloroform test that I shared with you that brought Lombardo into the case. I had an expert unlock Mr. Chen's phone and shared the contents of that with you. You have the nerve to suggest I'm withholding evidence from the police when you couldn't even recognize that a murder had been committed?" and then since Jill was in Italy she ended her critical analysis of the case by throwing her arms in the air and saying, "Mamma Mia."

When she looked over at her team, she saw Angela with her head down trying not to smile, while Marie coughed to disguise a chuckle. Brenda was just wide-eyed watching the proceedings, while Nathan was uncorking wine in the kitchen portraying confidence in Jill.

"Yes that is true, but why were you interviewing various businesses today? You were following up on information that we didn't have," Rosso asked not willing to give ground up to Jill just yet.

"We were following up on Randy Chen's credit card receipts that we received from his daughter this morning. You told us that you were getting the receipts through legal channels. Are you saying you didn't do that? Are you saying that you didn't even ask the daughter for that information? What information do you have that you haven't shared with us?"

Rosso could see that this conversation wasn't going as planned. He'd bungled it at the start with the suggestion that they were criminally withholding information.

"All right, let's start over. You're correct that you have been cooperative. Perhaps all of you could meet with us at the Questura tomorrow morning? As you Americans say, "We'll show you ours if you'll bring your paper with you," Rosso said pointing vaguely to the butcher paper-covered walls.

Jill debated his request in her head. She didn't like working with these Italians. Culturally, she was having a hard time understanding whether they were placating her, or genuinely seeking her expertise. At the same time they could be chasing their tails trying to find Randy's movements on the island. Then something else crossed her conscious.

"What about the woman in the sedan? Any thoughts to who she is and why she's following us? Could your colleagues have placed two bugs on our car and not have told each other what they were doing?"

"No that would not happen. Besides we have only one model of tracker and that second tracker is not one that we purchase."

"Who else uses trackers? Would this be from the rental car company?" Jill asked.

"I doubt it. This is a small island and there's no need to do that, but I'll ask just to cross them off the list. May I see your rental car paperwork?"

Nathan opened his briefcase sitting on the kitchen counter and handed the agreement over to the Lieutenant. He dialed a number and after identifying himself as a police officer conducted a short but rapid conversation in Italian. Before he had even ended the call they could tell the answer was no.

"Do you have public cameras near the two businesses we stopped at yesterday? Traffic cameras or do stores have cameras on their entrances?" Jill asked.

"A few do, I will check," Rosso said looking at his watch and writing a note in a small notebook. "They aren't open at this hour so I will call in the morning. I'll hopefully have an answer for you by the time you arrive at the Questura tomorrow, shall we say at half-past nine?"

Rosso looked at Dr. Quint and her team trying to assess whether he had agreement from the group. Clearly, Dr. Quint was the leader and would make the decision as to whether they would show up at the Questura in the morning. At the moment, he didn't have a legal means to compel them and his threats in the beginning had been met with an attack, so he could only wish for cooperation. Still he spent a few seconds fantasizing about seeing Dr. Quint and her team driven away in a Carabinieri van.

Jill returned to weighing his request in her head. Jo would arrive later that evening, and while she wanted to spend time on the other side of the island of Sicily, she wouldn't be doing that tomorrow. Would Russo have the cell phone movements of Randy's phone and share with her? It was worth finding out.

"We'll be there at half past nine. What's the address?" Jill asked.

Rosso offered a car to pick them up, but they declined as the last thing they wanted was to be kicked out of their apartment because of suspicious police activity reported by other tenants of the building. After the lieutenant left, there was silence in the room then Nathan said, "I'm glad we won't be seeking legal counsel to get you out of an Italian jail."

Marie added, "You go girl!"

Angela said, "All you needed was a 200-year-old costume and a high soprano voice and we would've had a true Italian opera performed in our apartment. 'Jill' would not work for the title, so perhaps we would call this police tragedy, 'Polizia'."

Jill just grinned at their reactions, while leaning against the door. Then she jumped five feet forward, when there was a knock on the door, then she grinned when she heard a voice ring out, "hello!" and knew that Jo Pringle had arrived in Sicily.

CHAPTER 16

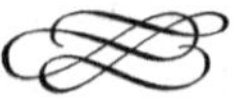

Sara dialed the long-distance number to the United States. A female voice answered, "Hello."

"This is Vice Questore Sara Cavallaro calling from Italy. May I speak with Melissa Chen."

Melissa recognized the voice and the name and replied, "Hello, detective, this is Melissa what may I do for you?"

Sarah was taken aback by the title detective, but then she supposed that was the influence of American television and the titles of police officers. She gave a few milliseconds of thought to correcting her title in English as superintendent, but it was not important.

"I wanted to provide you with an update on our investigation into your father's death and see if it's possible to obtain some information from you that will help us with our investigation."

Melissa was grieving, his death was so fresh. On top of that, her hands were full with managing the funeral arrangements, his company, and the realization that she was the executor of his trust. Furthermore, she'd been underwhelmed by the Italians. It was quite clear from the work of Dr. Quint that her father's death was not natural and yet if she hadn't hired her and her team, the

Italian police would have missed an obvious death. From her conversation with Jill, it wasn't just the head x-rays and the finding of chloroform, but even her father's position in the crater of Mount Etna should have raised concerns for the police. She would share whatever information the detective wanted, but she had little faith that the Italian police would solve her father's murder.

"Go ahead detective," Melissa said promising herself she would pay attention to the phone conversation despite the muddle she could feel in her brain.

"As you know, we have opened an inquiry into your father's death. In Italy, that inquiry is managed by a prosecutor."

Melissa couldn't resist, "Does he or she have any experience investigating murders?"

Melissa heard a sigh on the other end of the line and then Sara said, "Yes, as you may have read in the news, we have been engaged in a battle to prosecute the mafioso on the island of Sicily. They are the source of much of the crime that riddles this island, including many of the murders."

"Are you saying that the Mafia is involved in my father's death?"

"No. No this is not to say that they might be involved in your father's death, rather prosecutor Lombardo has experience with murder investigations."

"Are you working with Dr. Quint and her team?"

"That is in part why I am calling you. It came to our attention today that she was likely following up with businesses where your father shopped. She had information that we don't have, and we thought that perhaps you provided her with that information."

"Yes, she asked me for a copy of his purchases made in Italy over the past year. I provided her with a list this morning."

This phone conversation wasn't going well, Sara thought. They were so used to operating in a certain way in Italy, that when faced with a crime against a tourist they did expand their horizons to try new levels of inquiry. Why hadn't her team thought of asking the family for records of Italian purchases? How could she get the investigation back on track with this grieving family member of the victim?

"Dr. Quint and her team seem very qualified and on the ball. We should have thought of asking you for that same information. Instead we filed police requests with your father's telephone and credit card companies. As you can imagine, that's a much slower process to gain information. I would propose that at your convenience via telephone or email that we set up regular communication with you in the near future both to keep you abreast of what's going on and for us to explore the information you may readily have rather than the slower process of our legal channels. Is that acceptable to you, Ms. Chen?"

Melissa Chen was rolling her eyes on the other end of the phone. The Italian police officer's language was so formal. She supposed it was because English was not her first language.

"All I want is my father's murder solved, and his killer put in an Italian jail for the remainder of his life. If supplying you with information gets you to my goal faster, then I'd be happy to cooperate. I'm in the midst of funeral arrangements and estate planning. There's also the six-hour time difference. It would be more convenient for me to communicate by email. I check my email at least once an hour, so you'll get a fairly swift response from me unless it's the middle of the night."

"Thank you, Ms. Chen. Let me tell you what we're working on," Sara said and she proceeded to speak to investigating the transportation method of getting her father's body to the Mount Etna crater.

By the end of the phone call, Sara received an email from Melissa with the same purchase list that she had already provided to Jill.

Once they ended the call, Sara emailed Rosso and Lombardo with the details of the phone conversation and a copy of the purchases list. She went to work studying the list. Unlike Jill and her team, because Sara knew the island intimately, the names of the businesses and the cities that those businesses were located, it formed a pattern in her mind. She printed a map of Sicily and began making notations of the purchases in the various cities. She thought she noticed a pattern and it wasn't what she expected.

It appeared that while Randy Chen often stayed around the Catania area, he had a pattern of expenditures in the west area of the island. She drew an oblong circle with the city of Corleone on the east, Sambuca to the south, Santa Margherita to the west, and San Giuseppe Jato to the north. It was curious that he had so many purchases in this area of the island. Some of the inland towns were dying as the population moved away to the bigger cities of Sicily or for the mainland of Italy. Yes the towns were quaint, but there wasn't enough tourism to keep the residents employed. Why would he concentrate on this part of the island? Why didn't he stay in Palermo, which was so much closer to his area of interest than Catania? And just what was his area of interest?

She knew that he was an inventor of natural products to solve mankind's ills. She didn't know much about the fauna and flora of her island. Biology had not been a strong subject for her in school. Still she reasoned that likely different plants grew in these inland areas compared to the coast. She looked at the map again and decided that the whole area that he traced the route of several times was about 1,600 kilometers. That was a lot of acreage to be looking for a unique plant growing therein.

She felt a tingling in the back of her memory about something in this area. She closed her eyes and tried to recall what she had heard concerning this region. Nothing was coming to her, so next she tried the names of each of the four cities, concentrating. Again, nothing. Besides the four cities she traced on a map, there were perhaps another fifty to seventy communes in the area. Where could she start on trying to limit their area of focus?

CHAPTER 17

Jill opened the door to Jo and a hug. Jo ran the gauntlet of friends for hugs to find Nathan waiting with a glass of wine and a hug at the end. Jill pulled her luggage in from the hallway and wheeled it to the empty bedroom waiting for Jo. Marie introduced her sister to Jo. They had crossed paths some time at home in Wisconsin, but neither could remember when.

After a quick tour of the apartment, she flopped on the sofa, took a sip of the wine and said, "Whew! That was a long day of travel to have me here in person. I hope I give our client her money's worth."

"I explained that most of your work was on the internet, but this island feels like a step back in time, so maybe we'll find an actual hand-written ledger for you to peruse," Jill said.

"If you do, I would suggest that it's likely a scam by itself to keep a hand-written ledger in today's computer age. Hey Angela, how was the wedding? Was Mackenzie a beautiful bride? Was the wedding wonderful?"

"She was a beautiful bride. In fact after we're done discussing the case, I'll show you all the pictures. I got a new gadget for my camera that allows me to project the pictures onto a screen, so we'll just sit back with wine and Nathan's good food and watch the show."

"That sounds great. I'm amazed that a technophobe like yourself would make such a purchase. Could you also show me the pictures you took at the winery today? It would inspire me to see those pictures," Nathan said.

"There's a camera shop at home with people to help me make purchases like this and show me how to use it. It's come in real handy with the wedding. I showed the pictures the next morning to Mackenzie and her family and they were all in tears with the beauty of the wedding captured by the photographs."

"So what's the latest on the case? I distantly knew Randy Chen as I keep an eye out for local business leaders. I crossed paths with him over the years. I don't actually recall chatting with him, but what a terrible way to die and so far from home," Jo said relaxing on the sofa. "Have you guys eaten dinner yet?"

"Nathan's cooking for us and we were waiting for you to arrive before he started preparing," Jill said. "As for what's new on the case, step on over to the wall and we'll all give you an update. We're meeting with the police tomorrow at 9:30 in the morning to discuss our findings and they'll discuss their findings."

"You just missed Lieutenant Rosso's visit to the apartment and so we've been invited to the police station tomorrow to discuss findings with the State Police, the Carabinieri, and their prosecutor," Marie added with a grin.

"Somehow there's more to that story than you're telling me, Marie. What's on the menu, Nathan?"

"I have fresh fish and vegetables from the local market here as well as some pasta," Nathan added. "You're in for a treat, the fish is fabulous here."

"Actually I've never had a bad meal from you, so I'm sure it will be splendid. What can I help with?"

Jo spent a few minutes listening to what they had found so far on the case asking questions along the way.

"So we don't have a motive for Randy's death yet?" Jo asked looking for nods of agreement which she received. "So maybe I can help with the motive. Randy's death from what you have said doesn't sound like a crime of passion. We have no evidence that any family member or ex-wife had anything less than a cordial relationship with him, right?"

Again she got nods from her friends.

"In my mind that leaves two other motives - money or professional jealousy. I'm not sure how to run down the professional jealousy angle. That would have to be someone with insider knowledge of what Randy Chen was trying to develop or just someone jealous of the professional success of Randy's company."

Again everyone gave Jo a nod that they were following along with her reasoning.

"Let's go back to how the murder was carried out. Chloroform was used to knock him out and his body was moved by someone that had in-depth knowledge of Sicily. You would have to know the weather of Sicily, the location of the crater, and the means to find a way to transport his body to the crater."

Jo paused in her line of thinking to assure herself that everyone was following along with her.

"So I would conclude from all of those 'clues' that Randy's murderer is from this island and he was murdered to stop him from bringing this new product to market. It's the only motive that makes sense to my sleep deprived brain."

Jill agreed with Jo's reasoning, but her mind was going to the next logical step. How did they figure out what the product was that Randy Chen had his eye on? Clearly someone on the island had been alerted to Randy's interest, but how?

"I agree with everything you've said Jo and thanks for putting it so succinctly. Any suggestions on figuring out what the product was or who on this island didn't want Randy to develop it?"

"Yes, that's the ten-million dollar question," Marie agreed. "We've been interviewing merchants where Randy made purchases but so far have come up with only a bottle of olive oil."

"How about if we ask the question of why would someone not want Randy to commercialize a product here? Did someone want to protect the environment - was Randy planning on cutting down a forest for his product? Or did someone fear being overrun with people from Randy's company that would harvest this product? Or did they want to harvest the product themselves and use it as Randy planned or did it have another use?"

"This island has little industry and is the poorest region of Italy so I can't see that people would not want a future revenue stream. Randy's company is known for making environmentally sustainable products, so I don't think that would be a reason. Jill, don't many plants have multiple uses depending on their strength? Perhaps at one strength, a plant helps prevent blood clots, but at another strength you bleed to death? Wasn't Viagra developed for some heart ailment, but then company investigators discovered its use for men?" Angela said.

"Yes that happens with many drugs, but not so much with a natural substance although there are instances where that happens," Jill said.

Nathan had been listening to their conversation as he chopped herbs for the fish marinade he was making, so he called out, "How about Customs? Would Randy have had to take a plant back to his laboratory in Wisconsin to do some testing of a plant and wouldn't U.S. Customs have records of him declaring such a plant? I've known clients that have to get special paperwork to import grape vines for their wineries, so I would think it would be the same for Randy Chen's company's purposes."

Jill was struck by what a brilliant man Nathan could be at the exact right moment.

"Sweetie, you are so brilliant! Why didn't I think of that? Let's look up how you get an export certificate from Italy that the

United States will accept. I know that you have to prove your live plant is free from bugs and diseases to import. Brenda, can you have someone look through the company records for such documentation? I wish I knew someone in the Customs department to get that information from them, but maybe our police resources can run that down for us."

"I might be able to help with the customs contact as our company imports its fair share of plant substances," Brenda said, excitement in her voice that she could make a difference in the investigation of the death of her boss. She had felt so far that she contributed little, but maybe this latest detail might be the missing information they were looking for. She took out her cell phone with the intent of making a call to the company back in the states.

Angela had been looking up how someone gained an agriculture export certificate in Italy.

Jo was satisfied with her contribution to the investigation though it hadn't been in the financial realm which was her usual area of expertise.

Marie was taking to social media to see what people were saying online about exporting plants from Italy.

Jill wrote down Jo's comment about chloroform. Specifically she wanted to question the police about how a citizen went about obtaining that substance in Italy. Sicily might still use a chemical sister of chloroform for refrigeration and that might be the local supply, but she would check during their meeting tomorrow.

Nathan could be heard chopping additional substances for dinner and he called out, "Dinner will be ready in about thirty minutes and I have another range of wines for tasting tonight once we've eaten. Jo, we're trying to help Jill discern if she can grow and bottle the Nero d'Avola grape."

"I think I'll enjoy helping Jill with wine tasting as much as I enjoy finding a criminal on one of her cases!"

"So to bring a plant into the United States, the plant or plants have to come with a certificate from the country of origin that certifies the plant is free of pests," Angela said looking up at the group. "I'll find who issues such a certificate in Sicily. Brenda, on your end, maybe someone in your warehouse received a package from Sicily. Randy Chen was keeping this new product so low key, that perhaps only his warehouse and a chemist that tested the plant knew about it. I also wonder if a private company tested it and Randy paid for on his own account rather than the company's?"

"We can check the credit card statements from Melissa. She sent us everything and not just what was purchased in Italy, right?" Marie said.

"Yes she did," Jill said. "Thanks Jo, your line of reasoning on this case gives us a jump start on new stuff to research tonight. Let's split up the receipts among the five of us and each take three months to search for a potential receipt from a plant analysis firm. Of course he could have paid for the service with the company's account and Brenda, someone is researching that back home in Wisconsin right?" She saw Brenda nod in an affirmative. "Let's try the personal account on our end."

Once they divided the months of receipts up, there was silence in the room except for the occasional clacking of computer keys. They were all deep in research when Nathan called out, "Dinner's ready and I've already plated everything. Step up to the table, ladies."

There was a quick scramble as they noted where they were in their research followed by finding a seat at the table to 'ooh' and 'ah' over Nathan's feast.

"Not that I'm not grateful, but is there dessert? Just trying to pace myself," Jo said with a grin.

"Not really in the traditional American sense. There's gelato in the freezer, fresh fruit and cheese, or biscotti, but there's also the after dinner wine. So I've chosen to serve you ladies lemon water with your dinner."

"Thank you, Nathan, this is wonderful. It's like we hired our own personal chef in Sicily," Angela said as she said a quick silent prayer over her meal.

Everyone else chipped in with compliments, and Jill leaned over to Nathan for a kiss in thanks of the beautiful meal and thanks for being allowed to work on the case while he took meals off her hands.

Once everyone was sated and caught up on each other lives, Jill proposed a break for an after dinner walk and they soon set off on a walk around Catania. It was great to enjoy the fresh air and see the evening activity of the Duomo area.

Back at the apartment, Jill took a look at Jo and decided she was handling her jet-lag well and so they started on the flights of wine while viewing first Angela's pictures of the wedding and then the ones she shot earlier that day of the winery. After they finished with both the wine and pictures, Jo called it a night. Jill and the remainder of the team were anxious to see if they could find a receipt that would lead them somewhere in this case.

Brenda looked up from her phone and said, "There's no record of any plant arriving at our warehouse from Sicily in the past two years. Maybe Randy sent the plant directly to the chemist?"

"That makes me even more eager to find a payment among his personal account," Jill said.

"Wouldn't this kind of analysis be a purchase of several thousand dollars?" Marie asked. "I don't know what a chemist does, but it doesn't sound cheap. Perhaps we should concentrate on expenditures that were over a thousand?"

"I do my own plant testing, so I don't know the cost either, but I had to buy expensive equipment to carry out that testing so I would agree with your suggestion that we're looking for a bill of several thousand, or maybe multiple bills of five-hundred or greater. With that narrowing, that eliminates three-quarters of my receipts. Let's try Marie's suggestion.

"Bingo!" called out Angela. "I have two receipts for Central Wisconsin Analysis Lab."

"Let's call them!" Jill said. "It's Friday afternoon in Wisconsin and I would like to speak with them before they potentially close for the weekend."

"Okay, but let's think about our script," Marie said. "I doubt that a cold call is going to yield the information we need. Perhaps, Brenda as an executive of Randy's company should call. The firm can verify Brenda's identity on the company website."

"Good point. Let's lay out a script. Brenda are you willing to make the call?"

"Of course! I can see where this will lead us to new information about Randy's death. If my call doesn't yield anything, I will send in Melissa next to ask questions."

"Is she involved with the funeral today?" Angela asked.

"She may be making some arrangements, but the funeral is tomorrow."

They developed a script of questions to ask the company and Brenda punched the number into her phone.

The call continued for fifteen minutes as Brenda was placed on hold at times and other times she was taking notes. Silence in the room reigned from everyone else as each of them willed the answers to come across the phone. Finally, she ended the call and smiled at everyone.

CHAPTER 18

"The lab had the answers. Randy sent them a plant from Italy about nine months ago and I spoke with the chemist who analyzed it. Randy requested a complete chemical and biological analysis of the plant. She's going to email me the results to my work address."

"What's the name of the plant?" Jill asked.

"She gave me the Latin name and I wrote it done like it sounded but it may not make sense to you. The lab analyst said they did the genus typing of the plant and it's in the report."

Jill looked at Brenda's notes but it didn't make sense to her until Brenda sounded it out loud.

"Ah, like we discussed earlier it's from the oldenlandia adscensions family. I wonder what Randy thought was different about the oldenlandia adscensions plant in Sicily than elsewhere in the world? Despite it being in all kinds of products, there are no double blind studies that prove that it's effective at healing."

"The chemist was skeptical as well, but said that Randy didn't want the gel inside the plant analyzed, rather he asked that the roots below the soil surface be analyzed. He was thinking of using it for ingestion and wanted to make sure there was nothing harmful to humans."

Jill had been doing a search on oldenlandia adscensions as they discussed the phone call and said, "Ingesting oldenlandia adscensions gel is toxic and potentially carcinogenic to humans, but I know nothing about the root structure and specifically, I know nothing about why oldenlandia adscensions plants somewhere in Sicily are different. I need to do some research, maybe find an expert in the plant to see what they know of it."

"Did the chemist receive the plant, directly from Italy?" Angela asked.

Brenda hadn't asked the chemist that question directly and so thought back on their conversation. "No, she mentioned in the conversation that Randy gave them the plant in person as he wanted to meet the chemist to discuss the plant."

"Rats, I was hoping we could trace who was involved with the plant here."

"Maybe the police can trace that for us. Oldenlandia adscensions should grow nearly anywhere on the island except Mount Etna as it doesn't tolerate snow or frost, so we still have a lot of the island to search," Jill said. "I wonder where he found the plant - does someone own the land, or is a park? I mean if he was going to get sufficient quantity to produce an herbal remedy, then he would need to have the owner's permission to harvest."

"For some products, we grow our own plants in commercial greenhouses in the United States. We do that to control for purity and consistency. So my guess was that Randy would plan to harvest it himself back home," Brenda said.

Jill was stretched back looking at the ceiling trying to reason through what Randy was planning to do. Then her attention focused on the ceiling and she pointed to a corner and said, "What is that?"

Everyone refocused their attention and Nathan grabbed a chair to reach the spot in the ceiling. Jill handed him a tissue to keep his fingerprints off the item. He pulled on the object and it came away in his hand. He looked at it and then put a finger to his lips signifying silence. He then approached Jill's group and began writing notes.

'I think it is a listening device. I'm going to get the scanner we used to search the car this afternoon and run it through the apartment.'

They nodded, Jill pulled up an app on her phone with Heavy Metal Music and placed it next to the device, and smiled as she turned up the volume. Meanwhile they followed Nathan from room to room to see what else he found and they were dismayed. Jill put gloves on and grabbed some foil from the kitchen and soon they had a collection of devices collected from their luggage, purses, backpacks, and room ceilings. They would search Jo's room the next morning as there was no sense in waking her up to search her room. Besides, as her room had been obviously empty until she arrived, perhaps it was bug free. They were relieved to find no cameras as far as they could tell with the devices after they used a kitchen knife to disassemble one of them. Once they finished they wrapped up the devices in three layers of foil content so that the devices would no longer transmit and they could talk again.

"I wonder if we should take the scanner and walk down the street to see if there is a van out there listening to us?" Jill asked.

Her friends turned toward her with expressions of 'are you nuts' written on their faces.

Nathan spoke for the group when he exclaimed, "No, we're not going to do that. We're going to hand this over to the police in the morning. These bugs must have been placed while we were out today. Given the number of them, this is not just one angry person, there's an organization behind Randy's death. The only organization I know in this part of the world besides the government, is the mafia. You're not going to walk down the street and introduce yourself to them as they would as likely chloroform you and knock you over your thick skull and dump you into the Mediterranean Sea for fish food."

"Ah, okay I get your point, sweetie. I guess that was a dumb suggestion, but maybe the police placed them here."

"I don't think so," Marie said. "I don't think our favorite Lieutenant would have had a temper tantrum today if they had been listening all along."

"You do have a point. Okay, as it's late I would normally suggest we all retire to sleep, but I for one am too energized to do that. Let me go back to thinking about the plant, and what's so special about an Italian version of the common oldenlandia adscensions."

Her friends joined her as they were equally energized with the discovery of the listening devices in their apartment.

"Is the soil different here? Maybe the volcanic ash makes the plant different?" Marie suggested.

"That's a thought, but I can't find a variety of the plant unique to volcanic areas."

"Is there an Italian version of oldenlandia adscensions?" Angela asked.

"No."

"Could it be a new plant of some type - how do plants evolve or get invented?" Angela asked.

"Good question," Jill said pausing to look the answer up. "Okay it looks like about 2,100 species are discovered every year, but that mostly in remote parts of the world."

"There are parts of this island that seem remote," Marie said.

"Yes, but it's been trampled upon by Greek and Roman botanists, let alone modern day, Italian, British, and American scholars. It's hard to believe that any plant has been left untouched for centuries," Jill said. "Maybe it's a unique environment like soil constantly changing from volcanic ash. Should we ask University botanists about new plants in Sicily?"

"No! I'm sure the company would still like to manufacture

whatever product Randy had his eye on. If we discuss this plant with lots of people in Sicily, that opportunity will be taken away from the company," Brenda said.

"Brenda, are you sure that no one inside the company knows what this product is? I don't see how you can develop it if you aren't sure what Randy was going to do with the plant and what medicinal purpose it would serve."

"We asked all of our employees if they knew what Randy was developing and the answer was no from all of them. They knew Randy died so what's the point with withholding the answer?"

"Has anyone quit their job this week perhaps planning on taking the knowledge with them?" Marie asked.

"What! No one would do that!"

"I know you think that your company is full of wonderful people hand selected to reflect Randy's values, but then why did he go to such lengths to keep the product quiet within the company? Was he like this with every product, or was this one different? I mean I understand that he liked to meditate with each new product, but did he usually have an outside chemist do his testing?"

"I don't know the answers to your questions, Sis, but I'll find them. I can't believe any of our employees would steal this product idea," Brenda said sounding despondent at the thought of someone stealing ideas from within the company.

Two new pieces of information then arrived at the same time. Brenda received answers to Marie's question from the company personnel department and Jill received an email from her testing lab in Switzerland.

"We did have an employee quit this week. Her name was Stella Ricci and she worked in our shipping and receiving area for about four months. I have her home address here."

"Not to be paranoid, but that sounds like a good Italian name. Let's look her up in Wisconsin," Angela said. "I'll check in with some friends to have her identified."

"Hmmm, that's an interesting coincidence that an Italian sounding name was employed by your company, Brenda, but maybe it's not important information. My lab has some interesting information as well. I sent swabs of Randy's clothing and shoes to see if they could identify where he'd been. It's was a long shot and it's possibly meaningless information, but here goes. Randy had a variety of soils on his pants legs and shoes. Some of the soils reflect coastal Sicily, some reflect volcanic Mount Etna. He was recently in contact with moss spores that grow in caves in inland Sicily. Wow, I'm impressed with this lab as it was able to give me concentrates of each of the soil suggesting the degree of recent contact with each soil."

Angela's and Marie's faces reflected that they had their thinking caps on and were thinking of the various soils.

"Of the volcanic soil, did your lab specify which side of the volcano or is the soil the same all around it?" Angela asked. "It would be nice to knock off a section of the island because Randy hadn't visited it recently."

"Good question, I'll ask."

"Does oldenlandia adscensions grow in a cave?" Marie asked.

"It's a desert plant, so it likely would not grow in a cave. It's too moist an environment. That said, maybe that's our clue as to what makes this Italian oldenlandia adscensions plant unique."

Angela looked up from her computer and read, "There are four caves on this island and we can rule one of them out - it's the ear of Dionysius in Syracuse. That's a well-trampled tourist attraction, so I can't imagine any plants growing there. The Gelo cave is a part of Mount Etna. It's an ice cave formed by a lava tube, so this is a possibility. There's the Lauro cave just south of here. Finally, there's the Entella cave south of Palermo which is the biggest cave. I excluded any grottoes from this list as I assume there's too much water for plants to grow, but we can revisit later if these other caves don't pan out."

"Does the website that you're looking at describe these caves in any detail? We're looking for a cave that has lots of gypsum, so I think that means we can rule out any caves associated with lava rock," Jill said studying her report.

There was silence as Angela read the websites on the various caves and then she said, "I think we should focus on Entella cave, as Gelo is volcanic, and Lauro is limestone."

Jill was looking up the location of Entella cave on a map of Sicily and said, "It's just south of Palermo, probably about a two-hour drive from here."

"Their website says they're closed to visitors as they have falling rock."

"Let's plan on going there after we meet with the police. It will take most of the day, but if we go to the cave entrance we should be able to spot this plant, as even if it is a special oldenlandia adscensions plant suited to the moisture of a cave, it can't be far from the entrance as it does need daylight to grow and so we should be able to see it. I wonder though how Randy discovered the plant – I mean I don't think he would just walk around the earth and randomly spot plants that he wanted to use for products?"

"No, that's not how he operated," Brenda answered. "In some cases, the company made its own version of a product out on the market and in other cases he would be in conversation with a group of people and he would explore what you might call folk medicine. We would test the hypothesis that X product worked for a particular ailment. We might look for clinical trials somewhere in the world to verify the hypothesis and then develop our own product. So he went looking for this plant. We need to speak to whatever community he spoke with here in Sicily to find out what folk medicine solution he was after with the oldenlandia adscensions plant."

"There are several small towns close to this cave and then many more small towns if you back out to a range of say twenty-five miles. Hopefully, we'll find this community folk medicine soon or we might have to move to the other side of the island."

"That's a possibility. Marie, Angela, and Jo, you all have to leave in a few days. We'll likely need Angela's Italian to speak with people in smaller villages, but unfortunately I think we'll be seeing more of the Sicilian countryside than perhaps we wanted. I'm going to head to bed now and we need to be ready to leave here by nine in the morning as I think we can walk to the Questura."

CHAPTER 19

Jill enjoyed the dismay in the Lieutenant Rosso's face when yet he met another new member of her team when Jo was introduced to the Italian law enforcement members.

"Is this your entire team, or will there be another American arriving tomorrow?"

"This is it. We have a wide variety of skills that allow us to solve crimes, so this is all we need," Jill replied.

Looking at the paper rolls in Jill's hands, Rosso put his hand out and said, "I'd like to put these papers up on our conference room wall so that Vice Questore Cavallaro and Pubblico Ministero Lombardo can view your investigation."

Jill handed them over saying, "They're numbered so post them in order."

Soon there was silence in the room as Lombardo, Rosso, and Cavallaro studied the sheets of butcher paper posted on the Questura's conference room walls. Jo had been brought up to date on the walk over with the new information on the two lab reports from the Wisconsin chemist and the Swiss lab.

Finally Rosso said, "You have new information from when I visited last night. Where did that come from?"

"I thought you were going to share information with us. Where's your murder book, or investigative files, or whatever you call the collection of evidence in Italy?" Jill avoided answering his question wanting one of her own answered first.

Rosso sighed and slid open a door at one end of the room covering a dry-erase board behind it. Taped to it, were several pieces of legal paper with handwritten notes on it.

"Did you make those sheets for us or is that how you do investigations in Italy?" Jill asked.

"We did those for you and us. We haven't tried this method before, so we thought we would see if we had new ideas to solve the case. Don't you Americans have an expression, 'When in Rome do as the Romans do'? We Sicilians are trying to be Romans," Rosso said with clearly a distaste for all things Roman.

This time the silence in the room was on the part of Jill's team as they studied what the Italians had prepared. It was a faster method for her team to see what information the Italians had collected. What she didn't know was if this was all the facts they had on the case.

Once she finished reading their information, she said, "Yes, we got a chemical analysis report from an analytical lab in the States where Randy Chen sent a plant sample to be analyzed, I also received a report from the Swiss lab on the swabs I sent them from Randy's pants and shoes. We received that information after you left last night. We were frazzled over finding listening bugs in our apartment and therefore worked a little longer on trying to solve the plant that he was so excited about. Fortunately, the United States is behind Italy time wise and we could make calls to gain this new piece of information."

Jill could tell her comments were like nails on a chalkboard, when Cavallaro muttered in Italian, then asked, "Tell me about these listening bugs you discovered. How did you discover them and what did they look like? Who placed them there?"

Jill opened her purse and placed the foil wrapped collection of bugs on the conference room table, making a silencing gesture with her fingers to her lips. She looked at the three investigators and when she thought they were done, covered them up again in the foil and returned them to her purse.

"I understand that foil prevents the transmission of signals from these devices. I was looking at our ceiling for inspiration on the case when I noticed the first bug. We then went from room to room with our electronic scanner and found the remainder of them. Interesting whoever placed them in the apartment didn't place one in Jo's bedroom as it was empty at the time they visited the apartment, but you should know we left those butcher papers up all day since we arrived. We will now take them with us whenever we leave the apartment. We detected them before our conversation about the lab and Randy's clothing swabs, so we know they don't have that information."

"Why don't you leave those devices with us and we'll see if we can do something with them," Cavallaro said. "Are your fingerprints on them?"

"No, we used a tissue to remove them, so that might smear any fingerprints that were on them. Do your Italian criminals wear gloves to commit crimes?"

Lombardo smiled at that question and said, "Yes they have watched enough American movies to know that."

"Tell me about the cell phone movement that you mention here," Marie said pointing to a note on one of the pages taped to the board.

"Yes we were able to get a report from an Italian telephone company that reported the pings that Randy's cell phone made. I looked at the last three months, but I will likely seek more data on prior months. There are dead zones in Sicily where his cell phone wouldn't ping, but I did make a drawing of where it did ping. Our victim spent a lot of time in this region," Sara Cavallaro said pointing to a map of Sicily on the wall. She moved a finger to indicate the area.

"The Wisconsin chemist report reports that the plant analyzed is from the oldenlandia adscensions species. The swabs from his clothing suggest he spent time near caves that grow a particular moss. Oldenlandia adscensions is a desert plant and normally would be incompatible with a moist cave. Randy thought he was going to have a blockbuster on his hands which puzzled us as oldenlandia adscensions as a folk remedy has already been exploited to the maximum, however if he discovered a new species of the plant with unique properties that would have made sense."

"How did he find plants? I see from his passport that he traveled extensively around the world. I assume that wasn't vacation time," Cavallaro asked.

"No, he'd spent time sourcing new products by talking to folks about what they used for healing in different parts of the world," Brenda said. "Randy spoke with people in Sicily to find this unique oldenlandia adscensions plant. Unfortunately, we don't know yet what he planned to market the product for. We need to find this same group of people and see what they said about their healing solutions."

"You can't tell that by looking at the plant analysis report?" Lombardo asked.

"No. oldenlandia adscensions by itself is one of the most over-produced and unproven products on the market. He wasn't a marketing fool and so he wouldn't have gone to this level of secrecy for a product he already sold in his store. He had a new use for this ancient plant and we don't know what it is."

"Your cellphone pinging makes almost a perfect circle around the area where the Entella cave is located," Angela said. "That gives additional evidence to the idea that this might be the cave close to the oldenlandia adscensions plant that Randy Chen was sourcing. Jill, maybe we could collect some soil close to the cave entrance and send it to your Swiss lab for comparison?"

Jill studied the Vice-Questore's map and had to agree.

"That's a good suggestion. Also if we focus on that area, maybe we could look at the individual pings of the cell phone to determine how much time he spent in the many small villages close to the park in which the cave is located. We still don't know where Randy was murdered and it hasn't rained since we've been here, but I think it would be a needle in a haystack to find Randy's blood at a murder scene as he mostly bled inside his skull. The 'where' he was murdered doesn't help us find his murderer so much as the 'why' he was murdered. I doubt he offended anyone in whatever village he visited, so I'm running on the assumption that someone else had plans to market that plant – that's what makes the most sense to me. What do you folks think?" Jill asked looking at Lombardo, Rosso, and Cavallaro.

"For the prosecution of this case, having the location would be helpful," Lombardo replied.

"Well, at least you know where the body was dumped in the crater. Someone could have simply buried him or dropped him off a boat out to sea. Have you found the source of whatever transported him up the mountain?" Jill asked.

Glancing around the room, she noticed expressions of distaste about her comments on dumping Randy's body. So she added, "Whoever disposed of Randy's body in the crater, did so through an elaborate set-up designed to fool the authorities into thinking it was an accidental fall. And the murderer did fool you. Sorry to be harsh with my words, but that suggests to me that they knew something about police procedure because the far simpler plan would have been to dispose of his body. Sure the police and embassy would have applied pressure to find him, but this island offers numerous locations to bury someone, and as I said he could have been dumped into the sea and have his body swept away by the current from Sicily. Instead this person had the planning skills and patience to stage the murder as an accident. The murderer needed the snow on Mount Etna to be a key part of this plan. This murderer was watching the weather forecast and had already had a plan in mind to get our victim somewhere away from his hotel room to be murdered. Furthermore, this is the work of more than one person. Chloroform takes around five minutes of breathing to work. Your average human would not stand there passively for five minutes with a cloth over his face. So at the point he'd been knocked over the head or someone restrained him. Once he was dead or dying from the brain bleed, it would have taken two people to move his body."

Again Jill was met with silence as everyone was contemplating her comments. She'd also probably angered the Italians with her comment about the murder escaping their attention, but facts were facts and she was done talking.

After the silence went on for a while, her team studied the few sheets of information on the dry-erase board. Jill's mind was shifting through where to go next with the investigation and so she studied the map of Randy's phone movement. It was sloppy for the murderer to have allowed the phone to continue to transmit.

"Are these individual pings on your map or if say Randy stood in one place for ten minutes, there might be two pings at the same location?" Marie asked Cavallaro.

The Vice Questore seemed to shake herself to move beyond Jill's comments and on to thinking about Marie's question.

"This map is simply the mobile phone pings. If there were two in one place, there is still just a single dot. I will take a second look and add time."

"Do you have a computer person in your department that could program a computer to construct the data in that manner for you? It sounds like a tedious way to track Randy Chen's movement over the past several weeks," Marie said.

"We might have someone that could do that, let me check," Sara said pulling out her phone to make some calls.

"We have someone who could likely do this quickly if he's available to take our call, " Marie replied thinking of Henrik.

Cavallaro paused thinking of the time and effort to persuade one of the department's computer experts. She decided it was time to cooperate more with these Americans, and so said, "Go ahead and contact your person. I'll send you the report and you can forward it to your expert. Let me know if he or she can't do it quickly or at all."

While Rosso and Lombardo frowned over her response, Sara added, "What? It will not hurt the case to have their friend do something that you know would likely take us a week, by the time we cajole the right people in the Carabinieri."

As Rosso and Lombardo continued to show their disapproval of her methods, Cavallaro went on to the next subject – transportation.

"We researched the vehicles that could take Mr. Chen's remains to the crater. In addition to the vehicle that you rode in, Dr. Quint, to reach the crater, I understand that there are also quads which I believe you Americans call, 'all-terrain vehicles'."

Jill nodded and Cavallaro continued.

"Many people own quads for their farms, wineries, and tourism. We checked the large vehicles that carry tourists to the crater and we're confident that none of them were used to transport Mr. Chen. Which leaves us with the quads. Our officers contacted some of the witnesses that waited out the snowstorm. We specifically asked them if they heard the sounds of quads and the larger vehicles while they were waiting for the weather to clear."

"Good question," Jill cut in.

"Well the answer was 'no', so not necessarily a good question. One of the witnesses mentioned seeing faint tracks at the crater before the snow melted, so we showed her the different tracks made by the two vehicles and she identified the quad. We then returned to other witnesses who also then remembered seeing the quad tracks before the snow disappeared."

"So we have the vehicle that transported Mr. Chen," Marie said monitoring her email, looking for the response from Henrik, who thought it would take about ten minutes for her data on Randy's cell phone pings.

"We do think we have it; unfortunately that doesn't get us much farther. We checked our records and there are over two-hundred quads registered in Sicily. We can test a vehicle once we have a suspect, but otherwise we can't do much more with that information at the moment."

Marie looked up and said, "Angela, do you have your projector attachment with you?"

"Send me what you want to be projected and I'll put it on that wall," Angela said pointing to the lone empty wall.

Soon they were all staring at a map of Sicily with different size bubbles representing the amount of time Randy Chen spent in each location.

CHAPTER 20

"Wow, Henrik thoughtfully colored the bubbles likely to represent where he stayed overnight, based on the time of the phone pings," Jill said reading the legend. "That's helpful or otherwise we would be chasing cities that aren't important."

"Look, it even has the ping location on the day of his death, and from there the trip to the crater. Whoever murdered Randy had no idea about phone pinging," Marie said pointing at the various bubbles on the diagram.

"I wonder why Randy spent so much time overnight in Palermo or Catania, yet traveled all over the island?" Angela asked pointing at two bubbles. "It would have perhaps been a better use of time to stay overnight. This also looks like he spent time near these villages."

Cavallaro said, "Yes those are the villages of Contessa Entellina and Campofiorito. So the question is – are these the villages where he spoke with Sicilians about their folk remedies as you called it, or is this where the plant grew?"

"The third spot he spent time was here," Angela said pointing to the middle of nowhere and glancing at her phone. "Is this a park, or farmland, or simply uninhabited? When I bring up this area on Google Earth it appears as though nothing is there but vacant land."

"Are any of the caves close to these cities?" Jill asked.

Marie studied her earlier list and said, "Entella cave is perhaps within a close distance. It's the cave that has been closed to the public as it is structurally weak with stuff falling from the ceiling."

"Remember the plant can't grow inside the cave, but certainly can be close to the entrance, but then how did Randy get the moss on his clothes if he couldn't go inside the cave. Do you know if the cave entrance is physically blocked by a barrier?" Jill asked of the Italian officials.

They looked at each other shrugging, "I've never been there, so I can't tell you. I will call the University to see who has explored the cave. Could there be more than one entrance?" Cavallaro asked.

"We don't need to go inside as our plant is not there. We just need to find the entrance or entrances if there is more than one. Would your contact be able to give us the geo-coordinates to explore the area?"

"I don't know," Cavallaro said stepping outside the room to make a call.

"Dr. Quint, do we want to focus on a cave or Mr. Chen's cell phone movements?" Lombardo asked.

"Both, they're connected. I think we should visit the two cities and see if we can find the folk remedy that Randy was interested in and we should find the cave so we can physically locate the plant. As a botanist, I'd like to think I'll recognize the genus of oldenlandia adscensions plants. I think that once we start asking questions in the two cities about a folk remedy, we'll get two responses – people will volunteer the information and Randy's murderer will hear about us asking questions and we'll be watched. Don't you think that's our scenario?"

Cavallaro had returned to the room to hear Jill's question, and she looked at her fellow law enforcement representatives while thinking back to the history of crime in Sicily.

"If organized crime is behind Mr. Chen's murder, I have no doubt that they will be clued into any conversations we have in small villages in the area south of Palermo. Since Mr. Chen's murder was so well-organized, my preliminary thought is that the mafia is involved," Cavallaro said.

There was silence in the room after the Vice-Questore's assessment. It was a sentence they all dreaded, but each of them had individually thought that was perhaps who was behind Randy's murder. They were all aware of how worthy an opponent the mafia was on the island of Sicily and how their own lives would be in danger. Fortunately, they were diminished in power from their peak, but still a worrisome opponent.

"So what are our next steps?" Marie asked. "Can we get protection from the police and is there an organized crime expert in one of your branches?"

Marie was scared of the word 'mafia'. Sure they had faced bad people in the past, but there was a difference between a single deranged killer and a large organization that had the power to influence lots of people in Sicily.

Lombardo spoke in a string of Italian so fast and emotional that only his fellow Italians could follow what he said. Angela shrugged indicating she'd been unable to translate what they said. Jill waited patiently for the Italians to speak in English about their plan, all the while thinking about what her team should do next.

Rosso left the room pulling out his cell phone and speaking as he left. Jill turned eyebrows towards Lombardo and Cavallaro asking with her facial expression for a translation of what had been said.

"Tenete Rosso has left to call the Guardia di Finanza. It is where our law enforcement resources directed at fighting organized crime are located. They have offices in Catania and so we hope to have them join our conversation soon. Angelo is seeing how soon they can get here. I haven't prosecuted an organized crime case and so can offer no expertise in that area," Lombardo said.

Lombardo looked up in surprise when Rosso returned to their conference room saying, "They will be here in under thirty minutes. Perhaps we should take a coffee break until their arrival."

Jill shook her head. She wanted to stay alive and ten steps in front of the mafia. They needed every minute of the day to solve this crime and get off the island. She was convinced they would be safe once they returned to the United States. She resumed studying the map of Randy's cell phone movements thinking about a plan for her team.

She summarized where they were in the case. They confirmed Randy was murdered and how, they confirmed he was chasing after a plant from the oldenlandia adscensions genus. He'd been hiking close enough to caves to get some moss on his clothing. They didn't know how he was taken up the mountain. They'd been bugged so their movements and their conversations could be monitored...and all of these facts added up to more than an individual being behind Randy Chen's murder.

"Can we hire our own protection? Are private citizen allowed to carry guns in Sicily?" Jill asked.

Lombardo and Rosso frowned at Jill and asked, "Why?"

"I want to visit the two towns today and talk to people. But I'd like some protection which we may eventually get from you, but at the moment, I'm idle and wasting my client's money. I'd like to start by hiring private resources and keep investigating and when your law enforcement resources can offer us protection, then we will rely on you."

Cavallaro offered, "Yes you can hire your own protection, and yes they can carry guns as long as they have obtained a license to carry a weapon."

Rosso could feel the case slipping away from him again as the doctor was planning to take off in pursuit of new information while he and his colleagues were just beginning to mobilize. He gave some thought of what he could do to stop Jill Quint and her team from running off on their own.

"Look why don't I arrange a police van and driver. We'll have a mobile office while we can continue to discuss this case, and yet move towards the two cities in question under full police protection."

Jill liked that idea feeling safer with a squad of law enforcement rather than armed security guards to protect herself and her friends. She nodded her agreement, and Russo again left to make arrangements.

Forty minutes later, Jill and her team were inside a twelve-person van with an armed officer at the steering wheel. The new arrivals from the new branch of Italian law enforcement were briefed in the first hour of the ride about the case and the Americans role in it. Jill stayed facing forward occasionally contributing to the conversation as these Sicilian roads were not straight, and she was doing her best to avoid carsickness. Angela was taking the lead on conversing and designing a script they would use to question the locals at the various stops planned in the two cities. Brenda was quiet and overwhelmed by the people and place she found herself. Jo and Marie were talking on their own about other things that they saw along the way. A robust conversation was taking place as one of the finance officers didn't speak English and so there was a lot of translation that was time-consuming. Jill was glad she had Angela aboard to track the conversation. She was occasionally texting her in the front seat to keep her abreast of any significant comments. Angela said in one of the texts that the Finance Police were suspicious of Jill and her crew, but Lombardo, Rosso, and Cavallaro convinced him of the error of his thinking.

CHAPTER 21

S alvatore Denaro stepped out of his villa in the city Corleone, Sicily, made famous for scenes from The Godfather which were filmed there. Now like most areas of Sicily, the commune was looking sad and deserted as people moved away from the island allowing their previous homes to crumble. Still he looked around with pride at the life he'd built, perhaps he'd spend some of his fortune to bolster the town. First though he needed to get rid of the visitor to his island that was threatening his empire, his family, and his fortune. He'd come up with a plan to rescue his town, his island, his family. He had a vision of being the head of the most important family in all of Italy. All he needed to do was set up his drug manufacturing warehouse on the back of his property where no one would bother with it. And then several villagers from a commune fifty kilometers away had spoiled his vision by telling his island's secret.

He'd developed the perfect plan when he heard about an American man talking to those same villagers. He was patient and watched the man on his travels around the island. When an associate in the agriculture office let him know about the application to send an oldenlandia adscensions plant to the United States, he knew he had to move in and stop him. He'd assigned two of his associates along with an initiate to take care of the matter. They did and the man's death was declared an accident. He didn't know any different until he'd received a tip from a funeral home of the arrival of an American doctor and the Carabinieri. The mortician had let him know that the doctor had moved the body to the hospital for x-rays and was overheard telling the police that the death was suspicious. Salvatore had to get rid of the initiate as he hadn't yet passed the initiation ceremony. His men followed the Americans and listened in on the conversations, and then the State had opened a murder investigation.

Looking out at the view of his territory he asked himself aloud, "Why did this plan that had so much promise, go to hell?"

He received no answer back from his lands. His men were tailing the doctor and a bunch of women with her, but the investigation was too far gone for him to shut it down with the doctor's murder. The Polizia and Carabinieri would continue even without the doctor. The only good news he heard from his men was they hadn't figured out where the man was murdered or who had done it. There were no links to him or the family. Also the doctor was puzzled by the plant, she didn't know or understand the man's plan for the plant. Better still, she didn't know his plans for the plant which was so much better than the American's.

For years, the word in a certain region was the wonders of the oldenlandia adscensions plant found near the Entella Cave. Women spoke of its wrinkle and skin cancer fighting properties, men spoke of how it enhanced their virility, and teenagers spoke of the plant as a stimulant that helped them stay up all night studying. Salvatore has assigned ten of his men to investigate. A month later they came back to him with the information that their wives looked younger and their sex lives had been greatly improved. None had been willing to try it on their children.

Salvatore was pleased with the information. He'd had his associates investigate setting up a facility that would make anti-wrinkle cream as a front and for money, while they would also make a potion that would sell on the black market to men for virility. His own accountants had estimated a potential one billion Euro market for the two products. His people would be employed, his family the most important in Europe. His reputation and income would rival those of the Mexican drug lords. Sicily would finally rise out of its reputation of the impoverished region of mother Italy. It was a grand plan.

Then the doctor arrived to spoil it all, but she hadn't discovered all of the secrets yet, and so his plan was to murder her and her associates as well as the police and prosecutor assigned. Sure the government would replace them and they would conduct a new investigation into their murders, but they wouldn't discover his plans for the special oldenlandia adscensions plant. He needed to protect his idea at all costs and he feared that the only person who might discover him was this Dr. Jill Quint. She was the top priority of business for his family to resolve. This time he wouldn't dump the body at the volcano, rather they would be killed and weighted down into the ocean off the coast of his homeland. Their absence would be noticed, but they wouldn't be found.

He looked over his shoulder when he heard footsteps behind him and the greeting in Italian.

"Padrino," the man said, acknowledging Salvatore Denaro as his godfather or head of the clan.

"Yes, Tommaso, what have you found?"

"The doctoro found our listening bugs and removed them. Matteo planned to replace them, but we figured they would just remove them again."

"True. Do you know what they have found, where they are going? Is the team ready to eliminate them?"

"Yes, we have multiple plans to eliminate them. At the

moment, they are in a police van traveling to Contessa Entellina and Campofiorito according to our source. They have a prosecutor and officers from the Polizia, Carabinieri, and Guardia di Finanza. There are five American women inside the van."

"Five? I thought there was only the doctoro?"

"She apparently has help. One speaks Italian, another seems to do internet searches. We're not sure what they are all doing."

"So if we blow up the van we will kill five Americans and six cops?"

"Yes," Tommaso said.

"We need to develop another strategy. Call your men off."

"Padrino?" asked a confused Tommaso. His Padrino had never called off a kill.

"We will be run to the ends of the earth by the American government let alone our own. We need a new plan. I will convene a meeting to discuss. Let me see how soon we can get our men here."

Salvatore had muscled his way to the top of his family through ruthlessness and sound, but bold decisions. He wasn't about to bring down his family over a short-sighted decision. He'd put the family on the path to a new source of income that would fund the next generation and beyond, improve employment and infuse new money all over the island. He knew that taking an entire van of people out was a quick fix, but it would have long-term consequences. In his mind he wanted to cull this Dr. Quint out from the collection of people and make her disappear. It would cut the head off of this investigation, but he would see what his men suggested.

Jill barely survived the trip to Campofiorito given the narrow curvy roads. She kept her eyes on the horizon determined not to vomit from carsickness. She was grateful to get out of the vehicle and stretch her legs and let her spinning stomach come to a rest. While Angela had designed a script to use when talking with the villages, Marie had been searching the businesses in the town to locate who they should talk to – they wanted to focus on pharmacies and physician offices and question people therein. Their plan was to split up into pairs with an Italian speaking person in each twosome. Jill had high hopes about getting information out of people, but in the back of her mind was a niggling concern that if the mafia was involved, would any of the villagers talk to them?

She had her answer five hours later after they had visited the two cities and were on their way back to Catania. Someone had put the word out not to talk to them. Despite the evidence of Randy Chen spending time in the two cities, not a single person admitted to seeing him. Any inquiries about folklore remedies for illnesses and they heard the exact same response – they used lavender to sleep at night and chili peppers to make a salve for pain. To a person, they all said the same thing. Jill knew they had been coached.

There was conversation in the back of the van that Jill was listening to with everyone reaching the same conclusion. Someone had prepared the villagers in the two towns and the only source the Italian law enforcement officials could think of was the mafia. No one else had the reach and threats behind them.

"Is there a particular family in this region of Sicily or is the island controlled by one family?" Jill asked of the group behind her in the van.

She heard a sigh from somewhere in the back before someone recited, "There are fifteen families in Sicily. Each of the families has various zones that they control. In the area we were just in, it was under the control of the Corleonesi family."

Marie said is a squeaky voice, "Corleonesi family? Is that related to the people in the movie -'The Godfather'?"

Jill heard another huge sigh and then a voice said, "Yes and no. In the movie, the clan was called the Corleones, but in reality there is no one with that name, rather it refers to the city that the family hails from. In the 1980s before we broke up much of the mafia on this island, they were a part of the Cosa Nostra federation which is a loosely affiliated gang organization. That federation is greatly weakened here mostly because it no longer controls the cocaine trade. That's controlled by a gang from the mainland."

"So how do we break through this wall of silence the villagers have around them?" Jill asked.

Angela looked up from her cell phone to say, "We already may have broken through."

Even Jill took her eyes off of the road in front of her as heads swiveled to look back at Angela.

"What do you mean? Did you just get a message?" Jill asked watching Angela look down at her phone.

"Yeah, I did! We stopped in this pharmacy in Contessa Entel-lina and while my partner was speaking to the pharmacist, I noticed an older woman shopping in the lotion area, so I went over to talk to her. I explained what we were looking for and she nodded but didn't reply, so I left her my email address in hopes she might say something."

"Why didn't you say something while we were there?" exclaimed Rosso. "I would have gotten the information from her then.

"I don't think you would have. She watched your conversation with the pharmacist, and then proceeded to lead me into a conversation about the products in front of her, all the while her eyes were expressive about something else. So I wrote my email address out for her and passed it to her outside the view of the pharmacist."

"Good work Angela!" exclaimed Marie. "What did she say?"

Jill looked back and everyone was leaning toward Angela trying to peer at her phone.

"Naturally it's in Italian, but I believe she wants to meet me tomorrow. She's going to take the train to mainland Italy and wants me to hop aboard in Catania to join her on the ride to Messina. This sounds like someone worrying about being seen talking to us. Will I have trouble getting a last minute ticket for the train? Someone must be bringing her to Catania as I don't think she could reach Catania by noon if she comes from the train from where ever she lives."

The van was abuzz with noise, half in English and half in Italian. Jill broke through the conversations with, "Angela, I think you should board that train with Nathan for protection. He hasn't been seen by any of these villagers nor the lady from the pharmacy, but he'll watch your back."

Cavallaro and Rosso wanted to assign officers to accompany Angela.

"Look I want my friend to stay safe as much as the next person, but from what I read about the mafia, you likely have leaks in your organizations. It's safer for the woman and Angela if they just take Nathan along for the ride."

"Who is Nathan?" asked Lombardo.

"He's my partner and he has a black belt in Hapkido. He doesn't look or speak Italian. He'll look like a tourist heading to the mainland – I'll even send him with a suitcase."

"That's a great idea, Jill," Angela said. "He'll do a fabulous job protecting me, and he won't scare away this contact person. What are the rest of you going to do? I think we need to look like we're still searching for clues. This woman needs to be protected at all costs."

"What other clues do we have to run down?" Lombardo asked looking at the officers from the finance division used to chasing organized crime. "I thought we were only visiting the two towns that we did and it seemed like we talked to all the people we should have so what's our next step?"

The leader of the unit had been discombobulated by the appearance of the women into the case. He'd never before worked with a foreign law enforcement group and these women were not even trained professionals in hunting down the mafia. They were such liabilities, and yet they felt confident to pursue any aspect of the case. They were far braver than the situation warranted. Despite his reticence he liked the doctor's plan for sending the Italian speaking American on the train. Sending a martial arts bodyguard with her seems like a good idea. He also worried that the doctor was correct in that they might have leaks in their various organizations.

"Let's spend the morning in a meeting as a group. We have a room in our building that we can check for bugs. After that we can split up into say five or six groups and head out for other cities in the region to question folks. Meanwhile, Ms. Weber and your partner can board the train. We'll need to meet the train in Messina as it can be a two-hour train ride north from Catania, but just over an hour by car. We'll be wasting a lot of time tomorrow, but I don't see how to avoid it," said Maggiore Leggio.

"Are they any stops along the way where I could get off the train if we finished our conversation?" Angela asked.

"Yes, you could get off in Taormina which will come about forty-five minutes after you leave Catania."

Angela has been typing away on her phone while the discussion took place inside the van. She tapped the screen a final time then looked up and said, "I just told my contact that I would board the train and be wearing a soft yellow jacket so she would remember my appearance. We're good to go now, and we just need her to show up."

Jill texted Nathan to notify him of the change of plans for the next day in case he needed to notify any wineries of a change in plans.

Jo suggested, "Marie and I have never explored Catania. How about if we spend the majority of the day being tourists. It should be safe and confuse anyone watching us. We're leaving soon so it would be nice to see something of Catania and we don't have anything to research at the moment."

"I like that idea." Jill agreed. "Why waste your time stuck inside a building when beautiful Sicily awaits. If we get new information from Angela's contact, we'll be researching hard in the afternoon. So, I think we have our assignments laid out. Angela and Nathan to the train, Jo, Marie, and Brenda exploring Catania, and the rest of us meeting somewhere in Catania tomorrow. It's the best use of everyone's time and should blow smoke at whoever is watching and listening to us."

Jill listened as a conversation took place in Italian, then she heard a question asked "What happens next in the investigation?"

Jill thought through the evidence in this case and listed the facts they had resolved.

"I don't believe we have followed the trail of the chloroform. There's also the transportation to sort out. We could also head to

Entella Cave and look for the plant and maybe set up a camera to see who else has an interest in that plant. Let's keep our fingers crossed that Angela's woman gives up the clues we need to resolve Mr. Chen's murder as anything else is much more difficult."

With these remarks, the van was largely silent as it completed its journey to Catania.

CHAPTER 23

Angela stood on the train platform jittery with a sense of anticipation. Nathan stood looking at his phone, suitcase at his side about 10 feet away. As promised she wore the soft yellow jacket. She went over the woman's features as she remembered from the previous day. She looked around the platform for her contact.

Cavallaro had indicated that the train likely contained multiple cars and Angela wondered if she should simply not board if she did not see the woman on the platform – maybe she boarded at another station or simply decided not to come. Out of the corner of her eye, she watched an older woman approach the platform. She focused and decided with relief that she was her contact. She watched the people around the woman to see if anyone was tailing her and no one appeared to be. She was wheeling a large suitcase that fortunately seemed well oiled. She was short in stature with beautiful olive skin, shiny brown hair, and a trim figure. Her clothing was neat and formal and Angela guessed her to be sixty to sixty-five years old.

She knew Nathan was watching the platform to see if anyone is following herself, but no one was catching his radar. He drove the two of them to the airport, then they caught a taxi to the train station.

Angela was startled when the train went into the station blowing her hair around her face. She watched the older woman surge forward and into the front door of the train car, while Angela and Nathan entered the back. Given the time of day the train was not full and Angela easily made her way to sit next to the woman.

In Italian, Angela said, "Excuse me, is this seat taken?"

The woman looked up into Angela's face studying her for a few seconds before replying in halting English, "Yes of course my dear. How did you like that face cream I recommend?"

As planned, Angela replied, "I used it last night and it was soft on my skin," feeling a little like she should be in a James Bond movie. Nathan settled two rows back. He could hear them conversing, but he could only understand the odd Italian word.

Angela leaned toward the woman and said, "Hi, I'm Angela Weber."

The woman replied, "I'm Sophia Carlucci. I'm on my way to Germany. Once I reach Naples on the train, I'll fly to visit my daughter in Hamburg where I'm moving permanently. It's colder there, but safer."

"You feel unsafe in Sicily? It seems so quiet and beautiful here."

"Sicily needs tourism so we work hard to welcome people, but under the surface the Mafia controls everything. They bought the people and this land and it will never get better."

Angela put her arm on the woman's hand saying, "That must be so hard for you. I can see you love it here."

"It is hard. I was in the pharmacy yesterday to buy my favorite lotion as it's made locally and I can't get it in Germany."

Angela thought maybe this was the special potion that Randy was looking to develop.

"What's so special about the lotion?" Angela asked.

"It's made from a local plant and everyone in the village uses it.

We put it on our young children and we've never had a case of skin cancer. We've had other kinds of cancer and my fellow Sicilians who don't know about this lotion have gotten skin cancer, but no one in the village that uses it ever gets skin cancer."

"That sounds like a wonderful product. You have it with you? I'd like to take a picture of it, just so I can remember what to purchase."

"That's all right dear. You don't have to pander to me. I know you wanted to know about this product. We all knew that, but we were warned not to talk. Mr. Denaro actually eliminated the man who told your friend about the lotion. One day he was in the village and the next we never saw him again. We were all warned if we said anything, we would find ourselves dead too. That's why I'm leaving. I can't live with that kind of threat. Besides, this is a great product. All of Sicily and Italy should use it."

"I'm surprised that they don't. Why is that?"

"We all used to make it ourselves to put on our family members."

"You made it in a pot like a pasta dish, but this was a lotion?"

"Yes. There's a plant that only grows in an area south of Palermo that you have to process when it's freshly picked. So if anyone took the leaves of the plant to the mainland, it died before they could make something with it. So while we've known for decades about the lotion, it's just been something we use here."

"Your daughter in Germany doesn't use it?"

"No. Because the product is not endorsed by a famous company or celebrity, she doesn't have faith in our folk remedy."

Angela had managed to send the text with the photo to Jill so she could get working on it.

"I guess your daughter's thinking there is much less sun in Germany than in Sicily so less opportunity for damaging rays of the sun."

"Yes, that is true my dear."

"I'll definitely go get some of that magic lotion. I live in a location with similar weather to Germany, but one could never have too much skin protection. So who is this Mr. Denaro and why did the town listen to him?"

Sophia Carlucci leaned back to look at Angela, studying her.

"Ah, you cannot know what it's like to be under the invisible force field of Mr. Denaro. He has spies everywhere. He knows what every citizen and business is doing his empire. And profits from a million small things. I've watched businesses go under, unable to pay his protection and then the island dies from a thousand small slices from him and his gang. I've given up. It's never going to get better. So I locked up my house which will just rot, packed everything I needed and wanted into the single suitcase, and notified my daughter of my pending arrival time in Hamburg."

Sophia paused to wipe away a tear and Angela leaned in to give the woman a hug. Her heart was breaking over giving up her island and having to start her life over elsewhere.

Angela offered, "Maybe I can help. Maybe my group can see Mr. Denaro arrested for organized crime, if not for the murder of your friend."

"I don't think so. Many of us lived in hope he would go down with this special task force or another, but no one can take him down. So I've given up, I just want to take this parting shot on my way out of my homeland," Sophia said with fierce resolve.

"You've already helped. We knew there was a medicine of some sort used by some people in Sicily that would be of benefit to the world. We were even sure we had the right plant for this medication. We just had not figured out how the plant was used, or for what ailment. Do you know why the mob wants the plant? Preventing skin cancer does not seem like it would interest the Mafia."

"Oh, it doesn't dear. They discovered another use for it. It can be crushed and smoked apparently. It gives you a high that some people say is as good as cocaine. Mr. Denaro has plans to take on the mainland mob with this drug. I've heard he says that he will be able to lift this entire island out of poverty. Of course, half the population will be hooked on his awful drug and their lives destroyed."

"One moment," Angela muttered texting Jill with this information.

Angela finished the conversation with Sophia and they had moved on to the older woman's memories of growing up in Sicily. Angela was watching the time knowing that the Taormina stop was coming up. The train was slowing down when a man exited the car in front. Angela noticed Sophia stiffen and then she said something low under her breath. The man continued toward them but before he arrived Nathan blocked the entry into the two chairs facing Angela and Sophia.

The man was nearly a foot shorter than Nathan. When he could no longer make his way closer to the two women, he reached for something in his pocket. Just as the man's hand exited his pocket Nathan let loose the quickest of jabs causing the man's cell phone to fly through the air. Angela scrambled over the seat grabbed the phone and quickly opened the window to toss it. She didn't want him calling for help.

The man must've gotten on at the last station to search for Sophia. She moved back to sit next to the terrified woman.

Angela leaned in and whispered, "He's my bodyguard and he'll protect you as well. Let's get off at the next stop and we'll get a police escort to the Naples airport. We will make sure you arrive alive and ask the Italian police to notify the German police so you have protection there. We could even move you all the way to Wisconsin as I'm sure Mr. Chen's company would want your expertise with the lotion. In fact, I could arrange that now if you want to skip Germany and head to the United States."

Sophia Carlucci was stunned over the series of events in the last ten minutes. She thought she was going to escape the mob, then she knew she was going to die before she reached Naples, then an American man came to her aid and now she was being offered life in America. She knew what she had to do – save herself and her daughter. If she went to Hamburg, her daughter would be in danger. By heading to America, hopefully she could hide in that big country and not be found. Eventually she could go to Hamburg after the heat died down. And she would help launch a product that would save people from skin cancer across America.

She took a deep breath and said, "I trust you. Send me to this place in America. My daughter will be safer without me in Germany."

Wow, Angela thought. She'd been spontaneous with her job offer, and Brenda had been very interested in the product and she hoped she could talk her into hiring Mrs. Carlucci. She nodded then began making phone calls when she was sure that Nathan had the gangster under control. Angela made one call to Jill while staying on the train intent on protecting the brave Sophia Carlucci. The mobster got off in Taormina, and no one joined their car and the train set off for Messina.

After many phone calls, and some help from the embassy of the United States in Naples and the Italian embassy in Chicago, Angela knew by the time they reached Messina, that Sophia Carlucci was safe and employed. They were met by the financial police at that station and they would escort Mrs. Carlucci to Naples. Brenda had made arrangements for her plane to be met in Chicago. They would handle some paperwork with immigration and then escort the woman to a new apartment in Green Bay, Wisconsin where she would begin a new life.

CHAPTER 24

I t had been a wild morning as the information began flowing in from Angela. Brenda had worked to employ a woman, she knew little about other than she had the secret to Randy's next great product. Based on Angela's description, it should be a blockbuster. Having the woman work for the firm as they tried to understand the plant and the lotion these Sicilian women were cooking up in their kitchens would be an adventure.

Jo and Marie had missed the excitement until Brenda needed Marie's help starting the process for a work permit for the woman. Jo was disappointed that she hadn't played a bigger role in helping to solve the case. While money was at the heart of it for the mob, there were no accounting records she could look at to help them.

Jill was amazed by the activity of the past hour. She had found the secret folklore solution that she'd been searching for . While everyone hustled to see Sophia Carlucci on her way to the United States, she had sat back and wondered if she could still solve Randy's murder? Was there someone responsible in the mob who ordered his death, and could she find the someone who actually carried out the orders?

While everyone went to work on Angela's information, she did a search on Salvatore Denaro. Knowing more about the mob boss might steer her in a new direction. She also wanted to visit the cave close to where the plant grew. Maybe they might find some forensic evidence near the plant that would link Randy's murderer, though Jill had to admit it seemed far-fetched, but she was going to try that strategy tomorrow.

Nathan and Angela returned in the early evening, confident that Sophia Carlucci was safely on a plane to the United States. After conversations with the company and Marie, Brenda packed her bags and met the woman in Naples to join her on her trip to Wisconsin. She would serve as the woman's escort to see that she was safely settled and helping the company fulfill Randy's dream of producing the skin cancer prevention lotion.

Marie and Joe would be leaving in about twenty-four hours to return home and resume their day jobs.

"So is our work done?" Marie asked.

"Not exactly. We were hired to find Randy's killer. We know why he was killed and likely who ordered the hit, but not who actually killed him. So while his company will get the product that so intrigued Randy, this killer will get away if we close this case now."

"So what you want to do tomorrow? It's not like you can go knock on the door of Mr. Denaro's house and ask him if he ordered the hit on Randy," Jo said.

"Especially after today's activities on the train," Angela added.

"I want to make one final attempt at looking at what I think is the site of Randy's murder. Mrs. Carlucci gave you precise details on where to find the plants. Let's all head over there tomorrow and look around. If nothing else we'll see more of the island."

Jill was looking at her friends as she suggested the journey. She could read that her friends thought her idea was a waste of time, but they were willing to follow her on this last idea.

"I can read in your faces that you all think my idea of visiting the plants is bad, but you're willing to follow me anyways. Thanks, I appreciate the support. We were hired to find Randy's killer and we haven't succeeded with that. I feel like a failure for not finding more information on Randy's killer.

"Wait a minute, I think you should celebrate all that you have achieved," Jo said. "Especially in light of finding Mrs. Carlucci and getting her on a plane to Wisconsin. She's going to be the key to creating an incredible revenue source for Randy's company and his family. Furthermore, you did find Randy's killer, you just don't know who in the mob did it. You may have to accept that they do things differently here and you got as far as you could go. I think you should be impressed that you managed to draw the Italian law enforcement in on the case – that's was no easy feat!" Jo said.

"Yeah, I suppose. This is our third case outside of the United States and I'll admit that the cultural differences of law enforcement agencies and boundaries always frustrate me. I know how to get things done at home, but everything is longer and harder here to accomplish."

"Do you think the Italian police will go after Mr. Denaro? Mrs. Carlucci mentioned the other murder, so they have evidence to follow up on. I would also think they should be deeply worried about another street drug being created. There are enough illicit substances in the world already. I would hunt the man down, destroy any manufacturing plans he had and perhaps go so far as to destroy the plants that are the source of this new street drug," Marie said.

"That's a frightening scenario with one mob trying to take on another via a new street drug. I would think this would have implications for the rest of the world. No one wants to see another drug like cocaine created and unleashed," Nathan added from the kitchen where he was busy cooking them another Italian masterpiece. "Ladies, if you would like to focus on something happier, today's wine samples have now breathed enough for you to begin tasting."

The four women got up and approached the kitchen counter where Nathan had poured samples of five more wines for the Nero d'Avola. He also laid out glasses of water and breadsticks to cleanse their palates between samples.

At the completion of the wine tasting, Jill said, "Since we've been here in Sicily, I think we have sampled roughly thirty to forty bottles of this grape and I think I have a good sense of what makes a good vintage. I think we have been more successful with the grapes, than the murder case."

"We've had more clues on what makes the best wines, than we have for Randy's murder," Angela replied.

That generated smiles all around, then Jo asked Jill, "Do you think as a botanist that the Italian government might make the move to destroy a plant that could become the next illicit drug?"

Jill thought for a while and replied, "I don't think so. If the plant is proven as a source of an anti-cancer drug, that value would far outweigh the worries about a new designer drug. Besides, I can think of other plants that are used for both legitimate and non-legitimate means. Take the poppy plant – even after five hundred years of use, the poppy is still used to create morphine and heroin. Granted it would be very hard to wipe all the poppy plants off the face of the earth, but there are many plants that straddle the line between good and bad. Can you imagine if we tried to eradicate grapevines because people got drunk on wine and did bad things?"

"Not in my lifetime!" Marie replied.

"So back to the question of what the police are going to do next in this case, what do you think is their next step?" Jo asked curious to see if Jill had figured out the Italians.

"They have to get at Mr. Denaro – he's been implicated by Mrs. Carlucci. I'm sure that during the police escort to the airport, that they took extensive interview notes which will allow them to identify who threatened whom, but Mrs. Carlucci had the will and financial resources to leave the island. I wonder how many of her fellow villagers are in a similar position? I bet the police are met with more silence unless a friend is killed and the villager is fed up and speaks up. From what I've read since we arrived, the silence around the mob is what keeps it alive and well. I also have to think the economy plays a role as well. With high unemployment, perhaps you need approval by or connections to the mob to get a well enough paying job; that would buy a lot of silence in addition to the death threats."

"Yes, I can see the economic incentives to stay quiet are enormous," Jo agreed.

"And just think, we're only dealing with a single mob family at the moment. I believe that there are five or six on the island. It must be hard to live outside of their orbit. I admire Nathan's winery for trying and I hope with his help, he can help them rise above it all here."

"I've taken pains to disconnect my work from your name, Jill, on this island. As you can imagine, you're persona non grata here. I created a new moniker as an artist to distance myself from my true name and yours," Nathan said.

"I hadn't thought about that. Isn't it hard to build a new reputation in this country?" Jill asked shocked that the impact of one of her cases would be Nathan's professional status.

"Generally, yes, but I've been making small inroads all over the island while visiting wineries. At first, I really hadn't wanted to generate any business here as my plate is already full and this is a long way from California. However after visits to about thirty wineries, I'm more anxious to help than I ever expected. These vineyards have fantastic grapes, and I think if organized, the wine industry could lift the economics of the entire island and I want to do my share to see that these growers get there through hard work, good grapes, and some marketing magic rather than through favors with the mob."

"Oh sweetie," Jill said as she walked over to him to wrap him in a fierce hug whispering love into his ear.

CHAPTER 25

Salvatore Denaro was again leaning against the wall surrounding his estate thinking about his future. A month ago, it had all seemed so brilliant. He had a factory being built, a ready supply of raw material, and a new designer drug about to be unleashed. His income estimates had been so high, he thought it would enable him to elevate his family above all others in Italy. Today he was tottering on the precipice of the end as the family leader. How had his fortune changed so fast?

He had his family meeting as planned. He and his men had discussed what to do with the American doctor. They thought they had locked the territory down with the code of silence. Sources inside the Carabinieri said they had nearly run out of clues. None of the villagers had talked with them when they visited Contessa Entellina and Campofiorito. The day was successful and the risk of exposure to his new product was low. Then at the last minute he'd got word from his contact that one of the villagers was meeting someone on a train and was going to tell all. He'd scrambled all of his men to all of the train stations in his region as well as posting people in Catania and Palermo. His man in Catania had been delayed in reporting back to him and by then the damage was done. The villager, an older woman, had escaped his net and was in protection and on her way to the United States. He could still reach her there, but he had bigger problems to contend with at home. He tripled the bribes for news from inside the financial police and met with his men late into the evening until he knew what the police knew. He was still safe but his drug manufacturing plan was at great risk.

The police would be searching for his manufacturing source and if they visited the building on his property all they would find was wine barrels and a bottling and grape crushing enterprise. In the ceiling of that building was a hidden drying area just under the roof where they could dry the plant's leaves. Then underneath a rack of wine barrels were stairs to an underground lab that would turn the dry leaves into a powder to be distributed for a high beyond heroin. He used migrant laborers from Nigeria to build the facility and then let his men dispose of them offshore in the Mediterranean when he was finished. He had no fear of news of his building plans coming from the depths of the Mediterranean. Now he was waiting to hear about the next steps of the police and the American. Even though the villager had presumably spoken about the plant, they still had no link to him concerning the death of the American, so he was watching to see if the Americans left his island within the next few days.

He smiled as he saw his scientist walk across his veranda. He was here to tell him about the final tests he'd been running on his new designer drug. The scientist had recruited some drug users from Naples and they were confined to treatment rooms in the scientist's lab. He had to figure out what kind of purity produced the desired high, yet didn't kill anyone. His new drug would go nowhere if it killed all of its users no matter how good the high was. He knew the scientist had lost a few of his patients as he dialed back on the strength of the leaf.

"Dr. Petrov, have you completed your studies?"

"Yes, sir. I have the concentration of the drug perfected. All ten recruits took fifteen doses and didn't die. I had one recruit die between the fifteenth and twentieth dosage. That sounds about right, no?"

"Yes Dr. Petrov. If deaths slowly increase after the fifteenth dose, that's fine. Given the cost of the drug and it's hallucinations, I doubt many users will still be employed and therefore have the cash to pay the going rate for the drug. How do they die?" Denaro asked, curious about a drug-induced death, and whether it could be traced back to his enterprise.

"In my research on higher doses, the patients died from heart attacks. The drug revs the body up, then the blood pressure increases, then the patients will blow a main artery and bleed to death if the heart attack doesn't get them first. So these addicts will look like they're dying from natural causes, rather than a drug overdose. Since this is a new drug, there are no labs in the world that test for the presence of it, so we should go undetected for a while before the authorities recognize they're dealing with a new drug."

"Excellent. How many kilos a day do you think your lab can make?"

Salvatore Denaro hired this Dr. Petrov with the understanding that once he perfected the formula and manufacturing of the plant he would receive an ongoing percentage of sales. Of course, once this was all in place, Denaro expected Dr. Petrov to have a fatal accident somewhere on the island. He would use the doctor's percentage to fund college scholarships for the children of his extended family.

"I've got two hectares of the plants growing which will be ready for harvest in six weeks. Meanwhile, we've dug out about one hundred plants located near Entella cave and that will create a small amount of advance drug. The drug will be ready by tomorrow for distribution."

"What form will it be in?"

"Based on my research with these subjects and other drugs on the market, I've made it into a quickly dissolving tablet that the user places under their tongue. The drug then hits in under five minutes. Brilliant huh?"

"That is great news Dr. Petrov. It will be easy to distribute and administer. So you will have samples I can begin distributing tomorrow?"

"Yes. I have a few ready to go today. Would you like to try it?"

Salvatore raised his eyebrows at Dr. Petrov and said, "Are you nuts? There's no quicker way to destroy my life and my family's profits than for me to try our new drug. I am better served thinking of a name for it. Since it goes to work so quickly, I'm thinking of naming it Veloce or V."

Dr. Petrov spoke English to Mr. Denaro as that had been the third language he learned after his native Russian, then Ukrainian.

"Does Veloce mean fast in Italian?"

"Yes. At first, I was thinking of naming it Spider for one of the Ferrari models, but that doesn't translate well into Italian, so I've almost settled on Veloce. I will be discussing later with my friends who will be selling it. I would appreciate it if you would bring what samples you have to me now as I have a meeting this afternoon to discuss the distribution."

"Certainly. Do you have any other questions? If not, I'll fetch those pills now."

"No further questions. Thank you for this excellent progress report. I'm very happy we hired you to develop and manufacture this drug. I see we'll have a long and fruitful relationship ahead," Salvatore said knowing it was a good idea to reinforce the doctor's ego.

The good doctor just grinned rather maniacally, then turned and left for his lab. Salvatore made a note to push up his execution date to as soon as they were ready with the drug's production as the doctor seemed deranged enough to scare even him. He kept his fingers crossed that he would give his men the order to get rid of Dr. Petrov before he harmed anyone outside of the patients he was testing this drug on.

CHAPTER 26

The various branches of the Italian police force had been in a huddle since the American doctor and her team had left their conference room.

"I've made copies of the interview with Mrs. Carlucci so everyone can see what she said," said an officer who returned to the conference room after seeing the women safely onto the international flight to the United States. Moments later there was silence as everyone read through the report.

Cavallaro finished reading, and looked around the room at others at the table wondering if they had any informants in the room. Too late now she thought, as they have already read the report. She should have thought of that earlier. It was something all of the branches of the government contended with – organized crime informants on the inside. She trusted Rosso and Lombardo as she had worked with them in the past and observed no leaks, but this larger group made her suspicious.

Rosso watched Cavallaro scanning the group and knew what she was thinking, 'Who in this group was in the pocket of organized crime?'. He watched faces and body language trying to guess who would sell them out, but he came up with no answer. Maybe they would be lucky and there would be no leaks, but he doubted it. That was evidenced by the man approaching Mrs. Carlucci on the train.

Lombardo was still the lead prosecutor on the case and based on what had happened on the train and the notes from Mrs. Carlucci's interview, they had enough to charge the man that threatened the two women on the train. It was somewhat minor stuff though, and he wanted more. He wanted an end to Mr. Denaro's family and control of a region of Sicily. He wanted to find his manufacturing process, and he wanted to prevent a new illegal drug from hitting the streets of Italy.

"Do we have a picture of the plant involved in Mrs. Carlucci's lotion and the future street drug of the Denaro family?"

"Yes, Dr. Quint shared it with us when she got the text from Angela Weber on the train. Let me pull it up," Rosso said finding the link from Jill and putting it on the wall with the room's projector.

Lombardo stared at the plant that had so much potential to do good and harm to Italy.

"I believe we need to search Mr. Denaro's holdings for evidence on the plant. If he's planning on manufacturing a drug, he must have a ready source. I can't imagine that he plans to send his men over to the caves each day to pick plants. Don't you agree?"

Rosso and Cavallaro knew exactly what conclusion he was heading toward with this line of thought.

"Would you like us to search his property for the plant?" Cavallaro asked.

"Not yet. Simply growing the plant is not against the law. We need to discuss how the plant can lead us to the manufacturer hub. That is against the law if it is the production of an illicit drug. So how do we do that?"

That was the focus on the room for the next hour as ideas were tossed out by everyone.

"Could we have specialized dogs sniff out the plant?"

"Could we use satellites to find the plant?"

"How about if we sent a drone or helicopter over his property to photograph it?"

Cavallaro had been thinking as each idea was tossed out and offered her own ideas, "How about we compare satellite images to see if any new buildings and crops have been added to his estate or nearby and how about we search for purchases of the equipment that one would need to produce an illegal drug. We don't know what form he plans to hit the street with, but it's likely to be some sort of powder rather than a liquid, I think. Could we speak to a pharmaceutical manufacturing company here in Italy to get a list of what equipment to look for?"

"Those are great ideas, Sara," Lombardo said. "Let's organize to do just that, but I would also like to get a dog in here that can scent the plant as that could be key in an eventual search of his property."

All of their branches of law enforcement used dogs in a variety of ways – search and rescue, crowd control and anti-drug. The dogs were specially trained to smell cocaine and heroin, but a new plant was another thing altogether.

One of the other men spoke up and said, "Our search and rescue dog Lupo is fantastic at following scents. I bet he could find the plant with a little work beforehand. I'll make the arrangement for him to arrive here with his trainer. I will head over to the cave to find the plant, and begin training the dog on it. Perhaps he'll be ready to go by mid-day tomorrow."

"I think it will be hard to find the plant in the dark, perhaps you'll have to wait until tomorrow morning."

"That's probably true, sir. But since it's a two-hour drive, I'd rather head out now so we can get to work early. I will try to find the plant tonight, but I won't waste much time looking for it."

"Very good," Lombardo nodded approvingly as the man stood up to leave. He liked the officer's attitude.

Another officer from the Finance Division offered to run down the drug manufacturing equipment.

"I feel fortunate that we don't have any pharmaceutical manufacturers in Sicily. That should make your lead on equipment much easier to follow," Lombardo said.

"Yes, but perhaps it's a small-time operation that uses basic high school chemistry supplies. I always wonder how a plant goes from being made into a lotion for decades and then someone crushes it and tries to swallow it or inhale it to see what happens. I certainly never look at plants, and ask myself if I eat their leaf will it make me high?"

Lombardo sighed and agreed, "You and I will never understand drug users. We're just too content with the here and now. As far as Salvatore Denaro, he likely doesn't use it either, but sees the potential for money to flow into the family."

After a few more assignments, they broke up the meeting. Lombardo hoped they would be raiding Denaro's estate later the next day, but he needed some answers to the questions he'd tossed out to the group. Otherwise, it would be like looking for a needle in a haystack.

CHAPTER 27

Jill and Marie were up early the next morning planning their day trip to the Entella Cave. The previous evening, they'd had a wonderful meal and wine tasting and the shared camaraderie of long term friendships. There was also the depression of the group breaking up with Marie, Jo, and Angela flying home late that day. Perhaps they would be lucky and find evidence of Randy's killer, but she doubted that. She would stay a little longer on her own to see if there were any other leads to follow, but this might go down in her record book as her first unsolved crime. That was a depressing thought, but at least there had been several positive outcomes from her involvement on the case – Italian law officials were tracking down Salvatore Denaro who likely ordered Randy's death, and Randy's company now had the expert they needed in Mrs. Carlucci to manufacture the product he thought so highly of.

They were planning to leave by eight as they had at least a two-hour drive to Entella Cave and they wanted to be back in plenty of time to make sure her friends made their evening flight out of Catania. It felt like a fool's errand to make the long drive, but at least they would see a part of Sicily they hadn't been to before.

As planned, they started across the A19, a four-lane highway that ran across the interior of Sicily from Catania to Palermo. It was an interesting drive and the freeway was lined with blooming oleanders. They passed many vineyards and olive tree groves. As they neared the northern coast they turned on to the A90 which allowed them to avoid going all the way into Palermo and headed south towards Entella Rock. They were down to a two-lane divided roadway that perhaps hadn't been paved recently in parts, and then the road deteriorated more when they turned onto to SS624 and climbed through the hills. The road deteriorated one more time when they made their final turn onto SP60 and found a mixture of rock, concrete, and dirt the closer they got to Entella Rock. As they climbed uphill, there were beautiful views of Lake Garcia that would appear as curves in the road changed. They parked their car and began the half-mile hike following a GPS coordinate to the entrance to Entella Cave. The path was hilly, covered in low green grass and with boulders strewn about. There were no other visitors that they saw in this part of Sicily.

"Good thing we're in a group. I feel like we have found a deserted part of the world after the zombie apocalypse," Marie said.

"You're not one to see zombies around every corner," Angela said as they all chuckled at Marie's comment. "Let me know if you see any real zombies."

"This should be a zen moment as we have no noise pollution, no people, and mother nature at her finest," Jo said placing her thumb and middle finger together, closing her eyes, and assuming a meditative pose.

"Just a reminder my friends, once you're done seeing zombies or finding your zen, we're actually here to find this plant or some bloody forensic evidence that didn't come from a zombie," Jill said with a smile holding up the picture of the oldenlandia adscensions.

"Spoilsport," Nathan said. "I like Marie and Jo's versions of this remote location."

"Well, we should be seeing the plant at any moment. I can't believe the villagers go to this extreme for one plant. Angela, would Mrs. Carlucci have had a problem with this hike do you think?"

"Funny, I was thinking the same thing. Certainly I didn't observe her moving slowly or otherwise limping so she could have made this hike, but I remember she said that the plant leaves wilted so fast that they couldn't be exported to mainland Italy. So it seems like you would have to walk fast off the mountain and right to the kitchen cooking pot or to however they process the leaves, I didn't think to ask her if they cook the leaves, or grind them up raw, or do something else. Maybe the villagers making the potion teach their young children to run up and down this hill."

Marie was looking ahead to where they were walking rather than down at the ground and she spied on the next hillside, what looked like the cave entrance.

"I think that might be our cave. There seems to be a sign just inside the rock. Didn't we learn that the cave is closed to the public because the ceiling or the walls are unstable?"

Everyone stopped to follow Marie's gaze, pausing to look at the hillsides.

"Is this the only way to reach the cave or can you walk up from Lake Garcia?" Nathan asked.

They stood looking around the area and then Marie replied, "It looks like you could walk up from over there," she said pointing. "Why?"

"Just curious. Does this cave have another opening?"

"If it does, no one has mentioned a second exit," Jill said.

"Why is it closed?" Jo asked.

"The walls are unstable. People used to hike inside up to a decade ago. I believe then it was closed," Jill said.

"Are there earthquakes here?" Angela asked looking around at the rocks.

"There are earthquakes everywhere in Sicily, but I'm not aware of any big magnitude quakes for this area," Jill said.

"So we might go inside and then an earthquake could bury us?" Jo said.

"It's a possibility, but I think it's likely due to the fact that the walls and ceiling are formed by gypsum, which is not the hardest rock. We're far away from the earthquakes of Mount Etna here, so I don't expect to feel any earthquakes. I also don't expect to go inside the cave. I'm not sure if they have the entrance blocked anyway."

"Is this our plant?" Marie called out while pointing to a low green plant on the hillside leading up to the cave's entrance.

They were soon gathered around the plant comparing the picture to the actual plant.

"Yes, I think that's it," declared Jill. "Let's walk around the area to see how many plants there are and while we're at it, look for anything out of the ordinary – metal, candy wrappers, blood stains, anything you wouldn't expect to find on a hillside."

They spread out looking for both the plants and anything out of the ordinary. Angela had her camera out taking pictures, while Nathan stood on the hillside watching the distance with something prickling his subconscious.

He saw no zombies, but he didn't feel the peace that Jo had on the mountaintop. He slowly moved his glance from distance spot to distance spot before his eyes slid back as though hitting the breaks. He could hear the ladies conversing behind him, but his focus was on what he saw in the distance.

"Angela, do you have a telephoto lens for your camera?"

"Yes, why?"

"There's something in the distance I'd like to get a better look at. Can you quickly set it up before I lose the object?"

At once, everyone abandoned their search for something unusual and gathered at Nathan's side.

"Something has been bothering me since we arrived. Like I forgot to do something and now I remember what it was."

Angela changed her lens from magnifying to telephoto and handed the camera to Nathan saying, "You likely need to focus it here," putting his finger on the knob.

He quickly did as Angela advised and focused; meanwhile Jill and Marie recognized what he saw. In this peaceful deserted place, there were two cars on the way up the hill to their parking place.

"Is it a group of thugs in those cars or tourists do you think?" Jill asked.

"There are four Sicilian looking men in each car. I see no official marking on their clothing or car doors. Ladies, I believe we are in trouble."

"Do you see any guns?" Marie asked.

Nathan found it difficult to focus inside the car as it moved around the turns in the road, but finally he nodded yes.

"I guess we have about twenty minutes before they reach this spot, what are our options?" Jill asked.

"I remember what was bothering my subconscious. We forgot to scan the car this morning for bugs. I'm guessing they are coming for us."

All five stood on the hillside looking for places to run to or hide. The hillside back toward the car had a few boulders to hide behind. The hillside toward Lake Garcia had few places to hide and they would be sitting ducks.

"Let's try the cave," suggested Marie. "I'd rather risk a cave-in then being shot by armed men."

"Do any of our cell phones work?" Jo asked.

They all took a moment and several had no service while Marie's phone had a single reception bar.

"Who should we call?"

"Let's try Rosso or Cavallaro as we won't have to explain who we are and why we care about the two cars. Marie, you call them, I'm going to look for a way into the cave. Does everyone have good battery power on their phone? It will be dark in there and we'll need to use the flashlight function," Jill said. Then added, "Sorry, guys, that I got you into such horrible trouble."

"We'll survive. We always do," Jo said. "The world needs us to continue solving murders and finding people justice. We'll be on the plane tonight."

They paused for a group hug except for Marie who was talking to someone on the phone. At least they notified the authorities of where they were. Angela thought about sending her mother a text to say 'I love you', but that would only alarm her and her mom knew she had Angela's love. They needed to move.

Nathan stayed as outlook but knew beyond a certain point of the hillside he would be unable to see the car and its occupants.

Marie closed her phone and returned to the group walking toward the cave entrance.

"I reached Sara Cavallaro and relayed out situation and position. They are on their way. Fortunately, they are not far away, but still it won't take us long to be dead. At least the police know where to look for our bodies."

"Not to scare you, but I think if they are carrying guns, they aren't trying to be subtle. I think they'll murder us and then dump our bodies in the water and let the current take us away, or weight us down with weights a mile or two offshore."

"That's an encouraging thought, Jill, thanks for painting the picture for us," said Nathan sarcastically.

"So will our bodies drift to Africa or mainland Italy or will we sink after a certain time?" Marie asked as they peered around the barrier at Entella Cave.

"Your body will float for one to two weeks and the flesh will be picked off by scavengers like birds. When it's just your skeleton left, it will sink by no later than two weeks after you're dumped in the ocean."

"You're destroying my zen feelings of twenty minutes ago," Jo said.

They'd all been whispering, not wanting their voices to carry. They arrived at the elliptical entrance to the cave. It was raised off the ground and had plywood and a notice in Italian that it was closed. Marie wiggled the plywood, but it seemed attached to something that didn't make it easy to shove aside. Nathan tried to wiggle it as well to no effect. He looked around for something to hit the plywood with and instead stood on a rock and gave the edge a few explosive kicks. They were noisy kicks, but the plywood soon fell away. They entered the cave which was almost in complete darkness after Nathan pulled the plywood back in place.

They all glanced at their phone screen preparing to turn on the flashlight function when Jill said, "There's a text here from Cavallaro saying there's a Carabinieri helicopter on its way to us. All we need to do is stay alive long enough for the cavalry to arrive. It will take another ten minutes from now," Jill said looking at the time to mark it.

"Let's head inside. There are likely bats and bat poop in here so watch your head and feet. As bats go, these should be relatively disease free, but they could flutter their wings at us if we get too close" Jill said.

"Better bats wings than bullets is my new motto," Marie said.

"Yep," agreed Nathan. As the tallest of the group he was watching the ceiling. "Jill, do you know what's inside here? Is there water? A place to hide? Chambers? "

"I've read a little bit about it," Angela said. "It goes on for about half a mile, and there should be places to hide along the way. Also I have a battery operated photocell for my camera that will light this place up, but it will also show the men where we are, so I would rather not use it until we are rescued."

With her last words, the friends all reached together for a final fist pump before descending into a dark only illuminated by the phone flashlights.

CHAPTER 28

After receiving the poor-connection phone call from Marie Simon, Sara Cavallaro called her colleagues to see who had the fastest method to reach the four women and one man. None of the branches of law enforcement initially had access to a helicopter. They had a group approaching the village of Corleone planning on searching Salvatore Denaro's property and they were the closest to Entella Cave though still thirty minutes away. The Americans could well be dead by then, either because they were killed by the thugs or the walls of the cave collapsed on them.

She put the call into the team on the outskirts of Corleone, they were in several vehicles and included scent dogs. The way gossip carried in both law enforcement and small villages, Sara thought that Denaro probably knew of the upcoming search of his property.

"Vice-Questore Cavallaro, would we not be better to send a helicopter to reach the Americans?" asked one of the members of the Corleone search team.

"All but one of our helicopters are deployed guarding the pistachio crops at the moment around Mount Etna. I think the airtime to move one of those helicopters would take at least an hour given how far they are from Entella Cave," Sara replied.

A small region on the northern side of Mount Etna grew a special pistachio crop that was grown nowhere else in the world that produced nuts every other year. The crop fetched a far higher price than any other pistachio nut worldwide and had been the target of thieves until the Carabinieri began guarding the crops at harvest time.

"And the last helicopter?"

"It's in Palermo for any emergencies there. If we move it, there will be no coverage for our largest city."

"I think you should request that helicopter, I think the Americans are in dire conditions on that mountain and their deaths would harm Sicily for years to come."

Sara wasted a few seconds thinking about it, and then agreed, a few more phone calls and the helicopter was dispatched to Entella rock with an estimated time of arrival of fifteen minutes. Given the time it would take to walk from any car to the cave, that might be enough time to save the Americans. She tried calling but got no answer and texted that information to all of the Americans' cell phone numbers that she had knowledge of hoping that one of them might get it. Marie Simon indicated when she called that her phone was the only one with cellular reception, but phones had a way of seeking reception all the time and she never knew when someone might have a few seconds of access to receive a text.

Her contact with the helicopter had assigned her a frequency that she could communicate with one of the officers aboard. They had lifted off and already exited the airspace above Palermo. Marie had reported eight men in the two cars and the information that some and perhaps all, were armed. Organized crime had never shot down a helicopter and this helicopter had five Carabinieri officers aboard and would be unable to fly all of the Americans together to safety, but should serve as a solid defense against the armed men.

Besides maybe the men were on a hunting trip and weren't at all interested in the Americans. Sara thought that was probably a fantasy on her part. She wondered how the men had known the American team was at Entella cave. Perhaps before they left their Catania apartment that morning, they didn't check for GPS trackers. She couldn't recall from any of the previous day's conversations that the Americans had ever said that they were going to visit Entella cave, so the leak didn't come from law enforcement.

She looked at her phone to confirm that she'd received no texts from the Americans. They'd probably be inside the cave by now with no cellular reception. Then she heard the pilot mention they could see Lake Garcia and the profile of Entella Rock and there was a rapid conversation of where to land. One of the Carabinieri had a description of the entrance and GPS coordinates of the cave and knew it to be on the north side of the rock. From their altitude they could see three cars in the car park with one man leaning against one of the cars. They also spotted two men outside of what was thought to be the entrance to the cave. The copilot was unable to locate a place to land that didn't have the potential to have the rotor blades potentially clip giant boulders. Instead they used a public address system to see if they could scare some of the men off. They added a smoke grenade to the mix knowing that would get the men moving and the wind of the rotor blades would clear the smoke fairly quickly for the officers to see what was going on and rappel down from the helicopter to the ground. After the smoke dissipated, the man standing by the cars had gotten in one of the cars and drove off, while the other two men were moving rapidly away from the cave entrance and back toward the car park. Good start, thought Sara hearing the situation described over her headset. Three men down, five to go.

Three of the five Carabinieri officers rappelled to the ground with an equipment bag. The other one stayed inside the copter with the pilot ready to return when help was needed, but they were planning to set down on a distant ridge that looked safe for the rotor blades. The three approached the cave's entrance and noted the plywood barrier was leaning against the wall of the cave. Pulling equipment out of the bag that they might need including a first aid kit, headlamps, and extra ammunition they had. A quick discussion of the dangers of using a flash-bang grenade in a fragile cave. They decided to leave it behind in the bag. With headlamps on they proceeded inside then stopped to listen for voices or sounds. They could hear the rumbling of male voices and what sounded like footsteps ahead. It was pitch dark. One of the men had been in the cave as a teenager and described the walls, chambers, and passageways as he remembered them.

"Should we announce our presence?" asked one of the men.

"I'm not sure we have a choice. It's dark and tight inside in places and our night-vision goggles won't work inside an area with no ambient lighting. We'll have to use headlamps to find our way in."

"Will we have trouble finding them? Are there multiple forks in the cave path?"

"There's only one loop in the cave. There are branches off the main path, but they are all dead-ends. There are places that we'll need our torches to see where the cave continues as it may be a few feet up off the ground."

The men nodded and he continued, "I recommend that we go as far as possible and I'll lead. Once we get close to the other group, I will turn off my lamp as I don't want to be a target and I'll announce our presence. There are five Americans – four women and one man and we believe there are five members of the Denaro family inside. Let's hope none of them is hiding behind us. Also remember, it may be damp inside so no tasers and any use of our guns could result in severe injury with bullet ricochets. For the safety of the Americans, we would be wise to ask them to leave the cave. If we can catch them outside we'll arrest them, but I'd rather take their guns off of them and have them exit and return to their cars. Okay?"

The men nodded and they set off with as much speed as they could muster in the dark and over rocky surfaces. They came upon their quarry sooner than expected. They arrived at the first large chamber where beautiful gypsum fairyland lit up by torches. Stalactites and stalagmites created hazards to walking. By the time they reached what their leader had thought was the final chamber, they had made up considerable ground on the men and could see their lights ahead. It helped their speed to have headlamps rather than torches or cell phones to light their way.

CHAPTER 29

The Americans entered the cave with Angela at the front and Nathan in the back as it was better to have the tallest people book-ending their group. As Angela had predicted, there were rocks they had to climb up and over to continue along the passage. Jill, as the shortest member had to be boosted by Nathan when she wasn't tall enough to reach. They continued as fast they could into the first chamber and then discussed their strategy. They paused a moment to look around the chamber.

"This reminds me of the chase through the cemetery in the Sounds of Music movie. Let's continue to the fourth chamber as it's the largest from what I remember from the map I saw. Once there, how about if we each choose a rocky formation to hide behind. It's either that or hide in one of the dead end passages along the way," Angela said.

They all stopped whispering as they thought they heard a distant noise.

"We better get a move on," Angela whispered. Sounds traveled in the cave and they thought they still had some time to get farther into the cave and hope for more time for their rescuers to arrive.

"Sounds like we have company," Nathan said. "Let's hope the Carabinieri are not far behind. I agree with Angela's suggestion. Let's work on hiding as soon as we reach the chamber, and while we're at it, let's grab some of these rock formations as weapons. Try and hide higher up in the chamber as you'll be harder to see. Aim for their light sources rather than their weapons, and hopefully they have the brains to recognize that if they shoot their guns, they are as likely to get hit by bullets as we are."

"If I recall the final chamber has two dead-end passages and one passage that loops back to the main passage. We should probably plan to hide in those and hope that they are high or at least behind some rock formation. Of course if they're too hard to find, we won't find them either," Angela said as she began moving forward.

On that somber note, they hustled through the cave, walking as fast as they could and even jogging in a few spots that allowed it. When they reached the last chamber by Angela's count they all quickly dispersed to the farthest reaches of the cave chamber with rocky spears in hand, turned their lights out and waited for the approaching Italian voices and it sounded loud as the men were making no effort to hide their presence.

Jill did a quick look around the chamber hoping everyone was hidden, but as no one had their lights on it was impossible to tell. As planned, Jo and Marie were hidden in one of the passages, Angela was by herself in another, and she and Nathan were in the third.

They saw the light before they saw the men. Their lights were bobbing all over the cave walls and when Jill peeked toward the entrance, she saw no guns. Perhaps this wasn't the men that they'd seen in the cars.

Then, as the men entered the chamber, they turned and she saw guns tucked into their pants. Apparently, someone in their group knew they'd needed to keep their hands free for the cave chase. They scattered around the cave looking for them while speaking Italian, so Jill had no idea what they were saying. Angela could understand she was sure, but their cellphones didn't work underground and so they had no way to communicate.

The tunnel had been cool compared to the warm Sicilian air when they first entered and in their rush to hide they'd generated heat, but now they had been still for a short time. The cold was beginning to seep into all of them, and if they didn't watch it, they would all soon have chattering teeth from shivering. Jill had her arms wrapped around each other while clutching her crude rock weapon in one hand.

They were all hoping for the appearance of the second group of lights signifying the arrival of their rescuers – the Carabinieri. Jill's heart stopped when she heard Angela's voice in Italian. They must have discovered her. She peeked from her hiding place to see if she could help defend Angela. She got up on her knees making her best softball pitch at the man closest to Angela.

The light went out close to Angela and she heard a man groan and say something in Italian and then there was a sound of someone crashing to the ground. She hoped it wasn't Angela. There were no more words from her. Jill pulled back into her hiding place as a light approached the area she and Nathan were hiding in. Nathan passed her another rock as he coiled tightly ready to kick out at anyone that got close. The light continued to bob and weave toward their hiding place as a man held his light down to see where he was stepping. At the moment the man passed their hiding place which was elevated about four feet above the floor of the cave chamber, Nathan sprang a single leg kick to the man's head. The light source which must have been a cell phone flipped down as the man dropped with a groan.

Jill whispered in Nathan's ear, "Two down, three to go." She had counted the number of light sources that entered the chamber. With two lights out it was darker inside the chamber.

On the other side of the room, they heard further grunts in Italian as another light source was extinguished by either Jo or Marie. Three down, two to go she thought, then she saw an additional light source enter the chamber and thought, 'rats here comes additional men'. Then a voice rang out and something was commanded in Italian. She wondered if this was the boss's arrival. There was momentary silence until she heard Angela's voice in Italian. Why was she giving her position away?

"The Carabinieri has arrived, stay where you are," Angela advised her English speaking friends.

There was a further conversation which no one but Angela understood. Then the two men carrying lights exited the chamber minus their guns that had been in the back of their pants. There was a moment of quiet, then the room got much brighter as lights were turned brighter. Jill and Nathan heard a rustling followed by a few more words in Italian by Angela. Then Jill was squinting over the sudden bright light that originated from where Angela had been hiding. All at once they could see the beauty of the chamber they were in, as well as two men lying flat and another one sitting against the wall holding his bloody head. Everyone else in the chamber was adjusting their eyes to the sudden illumination.

After a moment, one of the Carabinieri officers said, "Ladies and gentleman, I believe you can come out now. I am Tenete Greco of the Carabinieri. Are you injured?"

There was movement around the cave and Jill said, "We have an unconscious man close by. He suffered a kick to his head. We're fine but cold. Angela, Marie, Jo?"

"We are fine as well, cold too, and our man is sitting up and is dazed and we can still see a gun close by if one of you would step over here to take possession of the gun," Marie said with teeth chattering.

"I also have a man not moving near me, but I don't see a gun," Angela said.

They all moved to assemble in the middle of the chamber eyeing the exit. Jill introduced everyone while Nathan's arms were around her trying to warm her up. The officers reverted back to Italian, and Angela was smiling gratefully at the words. Jill understood why when thin foil looking blankets were produced from a backpack. The other officers searched the men for weapons, then checked for a pulse.

"They're all alive, but they need medical care. Giovanni, why don't you exit the cave and notify our chopper that it may be needed to transport one or two of the men. Also let the Command know that the Americans are safe and unharmed."

The man nodded and left in a hurry.

"I'm a licensed doctor in the United States. Let me see if I can evaluate and treat the men," Jill said as she walked over to the man that Nathan had kicked in the head.

The Carabinieri officer that seemed to have the medical supplies joined her as she kneeled beside the unmoving man. Jill checked his pulse and ran her hands over his body searching for lumps or bleeding. His pulse was strong and his breathing fine and there was no bleeding that she found, and so she said, "He's likely unconscious from a concussion. He needs to be transported to a hospital, but he's not in such bad shape that he needs to go by helicopter."

She moved on to the second man and found blood on the side of his head, likely where her softball pitch with the rock had struck him. She heard him groan. His pulse was strong and his breathing fine, so she gave the same advice on hospital transport as the first man.

The third man's eyes were open and he looked suspicious when Jill approached. He had his hands on his head as though it hurt. His pulse and respirations seemed fine and she pronounced him fit to go to the hospital by ambulance.

In the end, they took the man who had yet to regain consciousness by helicopter to Palermo. Once more help arrived by car from the Carabinieri, they were able to use litters to move the men out of the cave. After statements were taken, Jill and her friends were cleared to return to Catania and would make it in time for Jo, Marie, and Angela to catch their flights. Jill wondered if the men would be arrested for their behavior in the cave and whether the officers would pursue identifying the other men that had gotten away. Frankly, she didn't care if she ever heard back from the Carabinieri about the five men that entered the cave. She and her friends were safe and uninjured and that was good enough. The man that had suffered Nathan's kick might have diminished capacity once he woke up.

The laid back life of Sicily had a way of growing on you, and Jill accepted the existence of organized crime and the fact that they were able to do so many unlawful things.

CHAPTER 30

Jill and Nathan were lounging on the sofa in their now empty Catania apartment. They dropped their friends off at the airport and they were on their way back to the United States. Jill had taken a moment to speak with Melissa Chen earlier about what they found so far and where the investigation was going. Melissa had heard much of the story from Brenda and Mrs. Carlucci upon meeting them in Wisconsin. Today's adventures were another chapter in the strange story of the pursuit of a skin cancer remedy. Jill told her that she doubted she would find Randy's murderer as there were so many organized crime members and so many places around Sicily were Randy could have been murdered. Melissa was pleased to hear that the police were searching Salvatore Denaro's property for the lab and manufacturing facility that would make a new illicit drug, but that seemed all Jill was going to be able to do for the Chen family. She and Melissa agreed she would stay on an additional two days to make sure no new evidence came from the search of Mr. Denaro's property. Melissa was fairly sure that once Jill left Sicily, she would receive few updates on the investigation into her father's murder by the Italian police.

Angela had left her a flash drive with all of the photos she'd taken since her arrival in Sicily. Now with a large glass of her favorite Nero d'Avola wine, she and Nathan flipped through the pictures on her laptop. Nathan was pleased to see the pictures that Angela had taken at the vineyard. They would be perfect for the marketing copy that he needed.

Angela had left them with over a thousand pictures, and Jill was flipping through them pausing every now and again when she viewed an amazing picture. She halted the slide slow and backed up two pictures not realizing at first what she had seen.

"What?" Nathan asked staring at the screen trying to see what had caught Jill's attention.

"Oh my!"

"What?"

"Don't you see who is in the picture?"

Nathan stared a while longer than his memory sharpened into focus.

"It's Rosso," Nathan whispered.

"Yep," Jill nodded

"And he shouldn't be in this picture," continued with his voice low.

"Nope."

"Did we run the bug thing this evening?" Jill whispered in his ear.

"Yes before we left for the airport, but not when we returned," Nathan whispered getting up to use Jill's bug scanning equipment.

He ran it over the entire apartment, their luggage, and even inside the refrigerator, but didn't find anything.

"Do you think they have more sophisticated equipment than your scanner can detect?"

"I don't think so. They would have to have invented a new radio-frequency wave. Let's visually look for cameras and then maybe we should go out for a walk and call Lombardo or Cavallaro while we're out." Jill said in a low voice.

Nathan nodded and fifteen minutes later they found themselves carrying the laptop and heading for the piazza. When they were a block away from their apartment building, they began talking in normal voices.

"I don't think we were bugged, but just in case we need to be able to talk about that photo. Do you remember where it was taken?" Jill asked.

Nathan thought back to the order of the photos and said, "Wasn't it that second day after you and Angela visited the crater? No, I'm wrong, it's the day we went to the vineyard I'm going to help with marketing. We thought we saw a woman trailing our car, but maybe that was Rosso wearing a wig on his head? Can I just say I never liked him? I thought it was because he was short and seemed to have somewhat of a Napoleonic complex around me."

Jill smiled at his short person comment, "Com'on, maybe you're the freak of nature here being tall and all."

"Right. Who kicked someone in the head and now I have on my conscience that the man might be permanently disabled by my blow to his brain..."

"You know he was going to kill us. I have no guilt about unleashing you on him. That kick might have been the difference between all of us being alive and well at this moment," Jill said solemnly.

As her arm was wrapped in his, she felt him take a deep breath and sigh. The man would remain on Nathan's conscious for a while. Perhaps she'd check in with Cavallaro in a month or two to see what happened to him.

"In some ways I'm shocked that Rosso didn't notice Angela taking pictures. Perhaps because his head was tilted to the side, he didn't see her at the time. Or perhaps, he was hoping none of us would notice him in the picture. That strategy worked for several days as I had seen the picture before and I was there when it was taken and still I didn't notice him there."

The picture showed Russo in the background, across the street from the pharmacy they'd stopped and talked to the people therein. Rosso had never mentioned that he was close by when they were interviewing people in that town. In fact, he had specifically stated he had someone follow them in an unmarked car, but that he had been in Catania that day. It was the night Jo arrived when he stopped by the apartment and was an ass.

"So what if he is in the picture. It's not a crime for him to be there."

"Yes, but he lied to us and said he was in Catania. I wonder if he was ahead or behind us paying bribes to people not to speak to us."

"What does that matter now?"

"You know I'm bothered by the fact that we haven't solved Randy's murder. What if he's the leak to organized crime? What if he never researched transport up Mount Etna? Maybe he gave us false information to throw us off the scent."

They had reached the large pedestrian thoroughfare in downtown Catania. It was full of people strolling to and from restaurants in the area. Groups of women were walking and there were couples arm in arm much like herself and Nathan. It was a beautiful night and Jill and Nathan were perfectly attired to fit in with the crowd. It was hard to believe that six hours earlier, the two of them had hidden in a cold, dusty cave that could have been their final resting spot.

"Maybe his English isn't the best and he lost something in translation talking to you. He did tell us we had a tail, just that it wasn't himself. Didn't he send his buddies to our aid earlier today? He could have just let us be killed."

"That was Sara who came to our aid. Okay maybe it's nothing and I should go back to looking at Angela's pictures to see if there was anything else of concern."

Before they made a u-turn to return home, Jill slowly examined the faces of everyone in the square with them but didn't recognize anyone. Once they arrived back to the apartment, they again scanned for electronic devices that shouldn't be in their apartment but found none.

After resuming their seats on the sofa and refilling their glasses with wine, Jill resumed the slide show, studying each picture with renewed interest wondering what else she'd missed. One turn through the pictures and nothing got her attention although something was niggling at the edge of her conscious if only she could reach out and touch it.

She started the second round of picture examination and finally stopped on a picture from earlier that day.

"What do you think this is?" Jill asked.

Nathan stared at the picture and finally sighed, "It's called, 'a thing that will make us drive nearly three hours across Sicily tomorrow'."

"Yes," Jill said with a smile at Nathan's pained realization of what his day would look like tomorrow.

One of the pictures close to the cave entrance had caught the sunlight glancing off of it, but it looked like something metallic with a 'G' on it. Could it be a Green Bay Packers pin of some sort that Randy might have dropped there? She couldn't tell the color of the pin and the Georgia Bulldogs used a similar shaped G for their logo. But how many Americans had been near the opening to Entella Cave? It wasn't likely a top hundred visit destination for the island of Sicily. Still perhaps it was just wishful thinking on her part because she felt so dissatisfied with her investigation into Randy Chen's murder.

The photo was nearly one of the last pictures Angela had taken. Perhaps she hadn't followed up on the metal object as that was when they realized they needed to head inside the cave to get away from the eight men in the cars. Both their run into the cave and their rescue put thoughts of forensic evidence out of everyone's mind.

She took a photo of Angela's photo to use for her search the next day. Then she decided to start at the beginning of Angela's photos and enjoy the scenes from her goddaughter's wedding. Then she and Nathan had an early night as the adrenaline rush of the day had long drained away.

CHAPTER 31

Once again, they were crossing Sicily from Catania to Palermo and then south toward Lake Garcia and Entella Rock. Jill thought back to other cases she'd investigated and decided this might be her wildest goose-chase. This could be a three-hour drive to nowhere. Especially if the Carabinieri helicopter blades stirred up everything on the ground. The pin could have been picked up by the wind and tossed anywhere. However, it hadn't been able to land in that particular spot so maybe the piece of metal hadn't been disturbed.

Jill had been on parts of this highway several times since her arrival to Sicily and she saw something different out the window on each drive.

Her cellphone rang and it was an Italian number.

"Hello."

"Ciao, this is Vice Questore Sara Cavallaro. How are you today?"

"Alive, thanks to you. I forgot to call you and thank you for sending us the help that saved our lives."

"Yes, it was tense time until I received word that you were

rescued successfully with no injuries. Are you heading home today?"

"No, we're actually on our way back to Entella Cave to follow up on one more thing."

"What? I thought your friends left last night? What are you investigating?"

"It's Nathan and me as indeed my friends did leave last night. We found an object in a picture that Angela took yesterday and it looked like something that Randy Chen might have owned so we're going back to take a look. It's probably a waste of time, but I don't like loose ends."

"I'm not sure what you mean by it's something that Randy Chen would have owned."

"Sara, are you a fan of football?"

"Yes, I follow the Juventus team," she replied confusion in her voice as to where the conversation was going.

"So you have a shirt or something from the team?"

"Yes, I have a shirt and a cellphone cover."

"So if we found you murdered in Siberia, Russia and there was a Juventus women's shirt nearby, we might assume it's yours, right?"

"Yes,..." Sara was full of doubt as to where this conversation was going with the Americans.

"That's what I hope to find close to Entella Cave. If I'm right, I'll call you as you might want some crime scene people. If I'm wrong I'll text you."

"Ah, okay. Let me know."

Jill ended the call and Nathan said, "You didn't ask her about Rosso?"

"It wasn't something I wanted to ask over the phone. Also, you convinced me that it was no big deal, so I'm going to file that for now and if it becomes relevant before I end this case then I'll ask Sara about it."

"Did she understand your example with Juventus?"

"Given the doubt in her voice, I don't think so. Because she speaks good English, I forget to remember that she may not understand all of our Americanisms, so to speak."

Nathan looked sideways as they continued through the countryside.

Jill's phone beeped with the arrival of a text from Angela saying that the three of them had made it home and all was well. Jill replied as a second chirp rang signifying an email. Sara had kindly given her a status of the three men from the cave, mostly about their criminal charges which made Jill happy. She got to the end of the email and said to Nathan, "The man you kicked has a brain bleed. They put a drain in at the hospital and he's recovered consciousness. The doctors expect him to make a full recovery with a little more hospital care. Hope that relieves your guilty conscious."

"Thanks, it does. While I've defeated men in matches, I've never seriously harmed or killed someone even in self-defense. I'll sleep better knowing there won't be long-term damage to the man."

Jill patted him on the hand as they skirted the edge of Palermo, before turning south toward their destination, and in less than an hour later they pulled up to the same car park they had used yesterday.

"Do you think all of the bad guys are in jail?" Nathan asked.

"No, but they aren't tracking us today since we remembered to scan the car before we set out."

Again they walked up and over the hillside that was Entella Rock towards where the cave entrance was as well as the plant that might make Randy Chen's company rich. Studying the photo on Jill's cell phone they approached the area where they expected to find the metal containing the symbols of a 'G'.

Nathan pointed to the ground knowing not to reach out and touch, "Here it is."

Jill squatted down and looked at the item and smiled. It looked new and shiny. Indeed a 'G' as well as '100' was on the pin. It was a new pin as this was the 100 year anniversary of the Green Bay Packers. It was very likely to have been dropped very recently as there had been no rain in Sicily since they had arrived. It had to have come from Randy Chen as he was on the Board of that organization as a prominent community member and would likely travel with memorabilia. Still she would have a lab verify that his DNA was on it.

She put her head down and decided it was a pin, the type that you put on a ball cap. She pulled out her cell phone to take pictures, then called Sara and asked her to drive to the Entella Rock park as she had found potential evidence.

Jill then began walking a grid around the pin. She took a moment to examine this area of the reserve and decided this was about dead center of the oldenlandia adscensions plants in this area. What else might they find here? And then she saw a rag or a piece of cloth and again she took pictures. She leaned downwind of the cloth as she didn't want to drop her own DNA on the cloth. She sniffed several times and the smiled.

When she was done and was sure the evidence was preserved, she took a seat on the hillside while Nathan returned to the car to bring back a picnic basket. There was nothing more she could do until the officials arrived in three or so hours and in the interim she and Nathan may as well have a picnic in this beautiful region of the world where Randy Chen probably met his end.

They were snacking on an antipasto salad, cheese, bread, and sparkling water when Nathan noticed a helicopter in the distance.

"I hope that's the Carabinieri and not the boys from yesterday."

"Yeah, me too. We won't be lucky enough to survive a second attack by armed men."

They watched a helicopter with dark paint on the bottom and a white roof and tail get closer. Then they saw the words Carabinieri on it and relaxed a little. This was a friend. The helicopter moved off and having watched the operation yesterday when they took the injured man with them, they knew the helicopter would have to land in a place that was about a ten-minute walk away. They proceeded to pack up their picnic so it was ready to go back to their rental car.

Rosso, Cavallaro, and some other men walked down the hillside toward them carrying toolboxes.

Jill pointed to the two pieces of evidence and explained what they meant and how they might be used. Sara smiled as she now understood Jill's comment about the Juventus shirt and Russia which had made no sense to her earlier on the phone. The Italian crime scene technicians photographed the items and collected them for evidence.

"It's probably all in my imagination, but I swear that cloth smells sweet which is evidence of chloroform. However it's a liquid that quickly evaporates when it comes into contact with air, so I know that the smell is actually not there. However, whoever held it over Randy Chen's face should have left their DNA on the cloth, so hopefully your technicians can find a DNA match."

"We'll also do a DNA match between Mr. Chen and this Green Bay pin to confirm that it was his. We'll do another search of this area just to confirm that there is no more evidence here," Sara said.

"I wouldn't necessarily expect to find additional evidence. He had a bloodless death. I'm most hopeful about any DNA you find on the cloth."

Sara nodded and Jill leaned in and held out her hand, "We'll be leaving Sicily tomorrow, so this might be the last time I see you. I want to thank you again for getting the help we needed here in time yesterday. You saved our lives."

Sara returned the handshake and replied, "You are welcome. Save travels, Dr. Quint."

Jill and Nathan began the walk back toward their car. As they passed Lake Garcia, they heard the helicopter lift off. She had no idea where the crime lab was located on Sicily, if indeed there was one on the island. Perhaps all of their evidence went to Rome or another central location.

EPILOGUE

Three weeks later, Jill received an email from Sara Cavallaro which wrapped up the case. DNA evidence from the cloth and pin matched the man that Nathan had kicked in the head. Fortunately, he recovered his mental capacity, and a confession was obtained in time. The pin also had DNA evidence from both Randy Chen and his murderer.

The Financial Police made a second raid on Salvatore Denaro's property and discovered the underground lab with the help of trained dogs. The mafia boss and his Russian doctor were arrested and charged with a variety of crimes. Nine people were found in dire conditions apparently addicted to the new drug that Denaro was making. They had been moved to treatment facilities elsewhere in Italy. The Italian police were worried that someone else would come along and make this new powerful drug so they torched all of the plants they could find. At this point, the only known sample of the plant was sitting in Randy Chen's corporate greenhouse, but that was an American problem if the plant was ever grown outside Mr. Chen's business.

Jill had a final call with Melissa Chen to wrap up the case. She was satisfied that her father's murderer had been caught and charged by the Italian justice system. She also dropped a postscript that Mrs. Carlucci had settled into Green Bay and the company. She was a real asset and would help fulfill Mr. Chen's dream of selling a skin cancer prevention lotion to the world.

Angela was arriving in a few days strictly to work with Nathan on a few photography jobs. He wanted dedicated time with his new photographer to make sure she understood his creative process and for them to work together on the Sicilian winery job. Then Jill would see her friends in a few weeks in Canada where they were taking a leisurely vacation close to home.

Jill had arrived back in California with an order of Nero d'Avola vines to be planted on her land. After the vines were in the ground for five years, she would create her first vintage of the new grape. In their own ways, Jill and Randy were alike, both leaving Sicily with plants to further their business interests. In Jill's case, she'd make bottles of wonderful wine, while Randy would never live to see his future skin cancer prevention lotion.

The End

ABOUT THE AUTHOR

I reside in Northern California with my rescue dog and cat. I love to travel, play sports, read, and drink wine and beer. I enjoy the diversity of the world and I'm always watching people and events for story ideas. All of my stories are generated by my imagination, I don't use AI to write books.

If you would like to sign up for my bi-weekly blog and announcement of new books, please follow this link: https://www.AlecPecheBooks.com

While you're waiting for the next story, if you would be so kind as to leave a review for this book, that would be great. I appreciate all the feedback and support. Reviews buoy my spirits and stoke the fires of creativity.

Readers that sign up for my blog receive a free prequel novelette for the Jill Quint Series.

ALSO BY ALEC PECHE

<u>Jill Quint, MD Forensic Pathologist Series</u>

Time's Up (prequel short story)

Vials

Chocolate Diamonds

A Breck Death

Death On A Green

A Taxing Death

Murder At The Podium

Castle Killing

Crescent City Murder

Sicilian Murder

Opus Murder

Forensic Murder

Return to the Scene of the Crime (short story)

Embers of Murder

Ashes to Murder

Mint Death

<u>Damian Green Series</u>

Red Rock Island

Willow Glen Heist

The Girl From Diana Park

Evergreen Valley Murder

Long Delayed Justice

<u>Michelle Watson Series</u>

Now You Don't See Me

Where Did She Go?

How Did She Get There?

<u>Dog Humor</u>

Eat, Play, Poop: Letters to my parents from camp

<u>New Urban Fantasy Series - Stephanie Jones</u>

The Awakening at Lake Tahoe (short story)

Witch's Medicine (2024)